Sts

Cozy Mystery Series Book 17

Hope Callaghan

hopecallaghan.com
Copyright © 2017
All rights reserved.

**Visit my website for new releases and special offers:
hopecallaghan.com**

Thank you, Peggy H., Cindi G., Jean P., Barbara W. and Wanda D. for taking the time to preview *Stranger Among Us,* for the extra sets of eyes and for catching all my mistakes.

A special thanks to my reader review team: Alice, Amary, Barbara, Becky, Becky B, Brinda, Cassie, Christina, Debbie, Denota, Devan, Grace, Jan, Jo-Ann, Joeline, Joyce, Jean K., Jean M., Kathy, Lynne, Megan, Melda, Kat, Linda, Lynne, Pat, Patsy, Paula, Renate, Rita, Rita P, Shelba, Tamara, Valerie and Vicki.

i

CONTENTS

Cast of Characters iii

Chapter 1 1

Chapter 2 21

Chapter 3 34

Chapter 4 49

Chapter 5 61

Chapter 6 72

Chapter 7 87

Chapter 8 98

Chapter 9 114

Chapter 10 127

Chapter 11 145

Chapter 12 155

Chapter 13 172

Chapter 14 189

Chapter 15 199

Chapter 16 214

Chapter 17 232

Chapter 18 246

Chapter 19 261

Chapter 20 273

Chapter 21 282

Get Free Books and More 295

Meet the Author 296

Gloria's Breakfast Bomb Recipe 297

Cast of Characters

Gloria Rutherford-Kennedy. Recently remarried, Gloria is the ringleader of her merry band of friends. She lives on a farm on the outskirts of Belhaven, a small town in West Michigan.

Lucy Carlson. Gloria's best friend. A bit of a weapon's expert and part-tomboy, Lucy enjoys shooting guns, riding four-wheelers and hunting...when she's not being dragged into one of Gloria's mysteries.

Dorothy Jenkins. Dorothy "Dot" Jenkins and her husband, Ray, are co-owners of Dot's Restaurant. The cautious one of the bunch, Dot would much rather stay on the sidelines during Gloria's adventures but most of the time it doesn't work out that way.

Margaret Hansen. Recently widowed, Margaret is learning to adjust to life alone. The most critical of the group of friends, Margaret tends to see everything in black and white with a tad of jaded.

Ruth Carpenter. Head postmaster of the Belhaven Post Office, Ruth is the queen of surveillance and is always up on the latest spy equipment. With her recently tricked out /

customized, bulletproof van along with her high tech spy gear, Ruth is Gloria's right hand gal in many of her investigations.

Andrea Malone. The youngest member of the Garden Girls group, Andrea met Gloria and the others through a string of tragic events. Despite the fact that Gloria is protective of her young friend, Andrea is usually in the thick of all of Gloria's investigations.

Love never gives up, never loses faith, is always hopeful, and endures through every circumstance. 1 Corinthians 13:7 (NLT)

Chapter 1

"No can do." Lucy Carlson shook her head. "I'm gonna have to pass on the raspberry twist."

"You're passing on your favorite pastry? Are you feeling all right?" Gloria Rutherford-Kennedy pressed her hand to her friend's forehead. "You don't have a fever."

Lucy swatted Gloria's hand away. "I'm fine. Fit as a fiddle, in fact. I figured at my age and now that I'm busy working on flipping houses, I need to get into shape and watch what I eat."

"Ahem." Margaret cleared her throat and raised an eyebrow. "And?"

"Blabbermouth." Lucy scowled. "The doctor told me that my cholesterol is a little high."

"Ah." Dot nodded. "Now you're making sense." She placed her Bavarian cream donut back in the box. "If Lucy can't have her favorite donut, then I'm not going to eat mine in front of her."

"I agree." Gloria had already taken a bite of her chocolate éclair. She wrapped the rest of the sweet treat in a paper towel and set it off to the side. "I could stand to cut down on the sweets, too."

The other friends, Ruth Carpenter and Andrea Malone, did the same. All eyes turned to the last woman sitting at the table, Margaret Hansen.

"What? I feel for Lucy...I do, but me throwing away my favorite donut isn't going to help her." She shoved the rest of the apple turnover in her mouth. "All gone," she mumbled.

"I have some gala apples we can munch on instead." Gloria grabbed the unopened bag of apples and the pot of coffee on her way back to the kitchen table. "At least the coffee isn't bad for us."

The women were meeting at Gloria's farm to go over the Garden Girls list of recent shut-ins. Visiting the shut-ins had become a juggling act the past few weeks, ever since Lucy and Margaret had taken on a house flip project.

Paul, Gloria's husband, was in between part-time security jobs and the couple was focusing on fixing up his farm.

Business was booming at Dot's Restaurant now that Belhaven Corners, a new neighborhood, was starting to fill up with families.

In fact, it had gotten so busy, Dot and her husband, Ray, were tossing around the idea of purchasing an empty building next door to their restaurant to expand.

Gloria set the bag of apples in the middle of her kitchen table and began filling coffee cups.

"Only a third cup of coffee for me," Lucy said.

"Are you cutting down on coffee too?" Gloria asked.

"I hope not," Ruth grumbled. "I don't mind passing on a donut or two in the spirit of being a team player but I have to have my coffee."

"No. I can drink all the coffee I want." Lucy reached inside her purse and pulled out a small container of sugar. She popped the top and filled the cup to half-full.

"Now all I need is a little creamer." She fumbled around inside her purse, pulled out a plastic bottle of extra sweet and creamy creamer and finished filling her cup until the coffee turned light brown.

"Just gonna give it a little stir." Lucy spun her spoon inside the cup and then sipped the sugary concoction. "I think it needs a little more sugar but it's close enough."

Dot reached for the creamer. "How many calories are in this?" Her eyes squinted as she studied the label. "This has 40 calories, 2 grams of fat and 6 grams of sugar, per teaspoon."

"It does?" Lucy snatched the creamer out of Dot's hands. "I thought it only had a couple calories." She slammed the container on the table. "Now I can't even have creamer in my coffee? What kind of life am I going to have if I can't even have creamer in my coffee?"

"You might as well have eaten the donut," Margaret said.

"There are healthier options," Ruth said. "I switched to a vegan brand with no calories or sugar."

"Gross," Lucy groaned.

"Let's get back to business. Sorry Lucy." Gloria reached behind her, and pulled the pushpin that was holding the wall calendar before placing it on the table. "As we get older, we've all had to make changes. If you do a little research, I'm sure you can find an acceptable substitute for the sugar."

She slipped her reading glasses on and gazed at the calendar. "Now let's work on the shut-in schedule for November, which is right around the corner." The women discussed their schedules at length.

Ruth offered to take the first Sunday in November. Andrea offered to take the second while Margaret took the third and Lucy volunteered for the fourth. Next, they went over the list of those needing a visit.

"I'll get something to write on." Gloria hopped off her chair, grabbed a small notepad and pen from the junk drawer and resumed her spot at the table. She turned to Ruth. "Who is on the list?"

Ruth Carpenter, head postmaster of Belhaven Post Office, was responsible for supplying the women with the current list of shut-ins. "We can drop Eleanor. She gets out more than all of us put together."

"I wondered what Eleanor has been up to." Gloria tapped the end of the pen on the pad of paper. "Every time I stop by to check on her, she's not home."

"I saw her pink Cadillac speed through town this morning on my way here," Dot reported.

"S-she's driving?" Gloria asked.

"Yes, and I would get out of the way if you see her coming. She's driving like a bat out of you-know-what," Ruth said.

Dot snorted. "That's because she can't see the speedometer. I told her she has to slow down but she's convinced she's only doing fifteen down Main Street when she's actually doing forty-five."

"And Eleanor only knows that because Officer Nelson stopped her and gave her a warning," Ruth added.

"Oh dear," Gloria said. "Maybe we need an intervention."

"Before someone gets run over," Lucy piped up.

"Okay. We'll work on an intervention for Eleanor. Now back to the list."

Ruth rattled off the list of shut-ins, starting with George and Maxine Ford. Maxine's health was on the decline. She was bedridden and her husband, George, was her only caregiver.

Next in line was Al Dickerson. Al, who had recently taken a fall on his way to the chicken coop, was recuperating at home. Gloria had visited him several times, bringing him casseroles and cookies.

At one time, Al and Gloria's sister, Liz, had dated, but poor Al wasn't exciting enough for jet setter Liz.

Liz now lived in Florida after cashing in her share of some rare coins Gloria, Margaret and she had found in the Smoky Mountains.

Next on the list of visits was Stan McTavish. His wife, Gladys, worked at Belhaven's pharmacy. Gladys was out of town, visiting her sister, who had knee surgery.

Last, but not least, was Vanessa Hines, a clerk with the Montbay County Fire Department. Vanessa had just moved from Green Springs to Belhaven.

Gloria meticulously listed the area residents they planned to visit and then scheduled each of the women with the date they requested. "We had a bumper crop of squash, beans and a bunch of rhubarb I froze. I'll take this weekend since the rest of you are taking the Sundays in November."

It would work out perfect since November would be a busy month for Gloria. Her son, Eddie and his wife, Karen, who lived in Chicago, were coming for a visit.

Liz was also hinting at heading north for a visit, which meant two of Gloria's four weekends were already booked.

"Sounds good," Ruth said. "Don't worry about Vanessa Hines. She's not far from my house and I can run by there so you won't have to bother."

"Or I can stop by her place Sunday after the church crowd thins," Dot quickly added.

"I don't mind," Gloria said. "Everyone else is taking their turn and it's only fair for me to take my turn, too."

"It's not necessary," Ruth insisted. "Dot or I can stop by Vanessa's place."

Lucy shifted in her seat. "Why can't Gloria visit Vanessa?"

"She can." Dot averted her gaze and stared at her hands, a sure sign she was hiding something.

"Dot... Why don't you want me to stop by Vanessa's place?"

Dot laughed nervously but refused to meet Gloria's gaze. "I..." She shot Ruth a helpless glance.

"Spill the beans," Andrea said. "What is up with this Vanessa?"

"Well, she..." Ruth shook her head.

"It's just a rumor," Dot blurted out. "I mean, we don't know for sure."

Gloria leaned forward. "What rumor?"

"There's a rumor going around that Vanessa moved to Belhaven to be close to Paul."

"My Paul?" Gloria was confused.

"We don't know for sure," Ruth spoke rapidly. "Judith told me her cousin, Minnie, told her Vanessa has a crush on Paul. Since his retirement, she's been looking for ways to be close to him."

"So she moved to Belhaven," Dot added. "Pearl confirmed it." "Pearl" was Pearl Johnson, a Montbay County Sheriff's dispatcher.

"I can handle it," Gloria said stiffly. "Paul is my husband. Maybe we can work on finding her a boyfriend."

"Oh my." Andrea clamped her hand over her mouth. "A love triangle."

"It is not a love triangle," Gloria snapped. "Paul and I are happily married." At least Gloria thought they were happily married. "This is silly." She waved a hand dismissively. "We are all adults. I'll visit the shut-ins and officially welcome Vanessa to Belhaven this Sunday." Gloria changed the subject. In her mind, it was settled.

The girls chatted about local events, the upcoming holidays and all of their busy schedules. They agreed they would get together to celebrate the Thanksgiving holiday again this year.

Gloria thought it was especially important for Margaret, who had lost her husband, Don, earlier in the year. Lucy, who was also single but had children who lived in the area, would be alone too.

Ruth had never married and Gloria always included her in the holiday get-togethers.

Andrea had already let them know that Brian and she would be heading to New York to spend Thanksgiving with her parents, which left Dot, Ray, Johnnie and Rose.

The group was growing by leaps and bounds, and although Gloria's rambling farmhouse could hold a bunch of people, they would be bursting at the seams this year.

Paul and Gloria had come up with a brilliant plan to spruce up the barn and hold the Thanksgiving feast there. Since they would have ample room, the couple decided to invite some of the shut-ins, as well.

After the girls left, Gloria straightened the kitchen, her thoughts wandering to what Dot and Ruth had said. She felt sorry for Vanessa. Why would the woman chase after a married man?

Belhaven was a small town. Surely, the woman had to know word would get back to Gloria.

The rest of the week passed by quickly and Gloria never mentioned the conversation about Vanessa to her husband.

Pastor Nate's Sunday message was about forgiveness, preceded by a gentle reminder to the congregation that the holidays were right around the corner and a good time to practice forgiveness, especially with family members.

After the Sunday church service, Gloria and Paul headed home for a quick bite to eat. Paul was anxious to wrap up the final repairs to the barn now that they planned to hold the

Thanksgiving feast there. He hoped to get everything done before the first freeze, which could be any day.

Gloria finished putting away the lunch dishes and began gathering the rhubarb pies she'd made the previous day, along with a few loaves of homemade bread and garden vegetables.

"C'mon Mally. Let's make our rounds." Gloria and Mally climbed into Annabelle, Gloria's car, and headed to George and Maxine Ford's place first.

Gloria stayed long enough to drink a cup of coffee and eat a small slice of pie before heading across town to visit with Stan McTavish. Stan wasn't home, so she hung a bag of vegetables on his back porch doorknob and headed to Al Dickerson's place.

Al was waiting for Gloria on his front porch. He rolled his wheelchair to the edge of the top step as Mally and she exited the car. "I got a fresh pot of coffee brewing." He took the bag of vegetables and pie and set them on his lap. "There's nothing better than fresh coffee and homemade pie. You'll stay for a piece?" he asked hopefully.

"Of course." Gloria didn't have the heart to say no. "A small piece, though." She patted her stomach. "I'm trying to watch my girlish figure."

Mally trotted off to inspect Al's corncrib and Gloria headed inside to help Al. The house looked the same as when Cecelia, Al's wife, had been alive.

More than once, Al mentioned his children wanted him to sell the farm and move to a condominium development not far from his eldest son, but Al stubbornly refused.

Gloria secretly suspected he was concerned that if he sold the farm and moved away, the last remnants of the life he'd shared with Cecelia would be gone.

When they reached the kitchen, Gloria poured two cups of coffee and carried them to the table.

Al finished slicing the pie and slid a piece in front of Gloria before taking a big bite of his own. "You got this one just right. It's the perfect amount of tart and sweet."

Gloria popped a bite in her mouth and her taste buds tingled at the tartness. "I think this is one of my best rhubarb pies ever."

While they ate, they chatted about the weather and upcoming holidays. Finally, Gloria stood. "Mally and I better get going. We've got one more stop to make, at the home of Belhaven's newest resident, Vanessa Hines."

Al nodded. "She bought Joanne Gibbs place. Heard Joanne's kids moved her to the nursing home in Green Springs."

"Yes. The house was too much for poor Joanne." The large Dutch colonial had always given Gloria the heebie-jeebies and the house's third floor half-moon windows reminded her of eyes.

Lucy told Gloria she'd taken a look at the property as a potential second reno project, but it was full of junk, needed a lot of work and Lucy wasn't sure she was ready to tackle a project of that magnitude.

Gloria wondered why Vanessa, a single woman, would purchase such a large property, and one that needed major repairs to boot.

She told Al good-bye, herded Mally into the car and then drove back into town. When she reached Vanessa's place, she pulled into the gravel drive and parked behind a blue Buick sedan. The first thing Gloria noticed were the baskets of artificial flowers hanging on the front porch.

Gloria and Mally headed to the front door, rang the doorbell and waited. "Maybe the doorbell doesn't work," she told Mally, and then rapped sharply on the screen door.

There was still no answer, so she stepped to the side and peered in the picture window. The television was on but there was no one in sight. "Let's try the back door."

They retraced their steps and walked past the cars. Beyond the drive and off to one side was a tidy row of rotting pumpkins. "Looks like Vanessa is tilling up an old garden."

Mally trotted across the yard to inspect the pumpkins and Gloria climbed the back porch steps. She shifted the pie, along with the bag of vegetables, to her other hand and knocked on the door. There was still no answer so she twisted the knob.

The door was unlocked so Gloria stuck her head inside. "Hello? Vanessa? It's me. Gloria Kennedy."

She could hear the echo of the television, but there was still no answer, so Gloria carefully placed the pie and bag of vegetables on the floor.

Mally, who had returned to Gloria's side, bolted past her and ran into the breezeway.

"Mally!" She could hear her pooch's nails clicking on the tile floor. "Come back here!"

Mally barked but didn't return, so Gloria sucked in a breath and stepped inside. Off to the left, she could see a set of stairs, leading to the basement and a small movement caught her eye before disappearing from sight. It was Mally.

Gloria hurried to the top of the stairs. "Come here," she commanded but Mally, who had reached the bottom, wouldn't budge so she took a tentative step down and flipped the light switch on the wall.

At the bottom of the stairs was a woman, and she was lying face down on the cement floor.

Chapter 2

Gloria raced down the stairs and dropped to her knees. "Oh my gosh!" She pressed the palm of her hand against the woman's arm. It was cold to the touch.

The woman was sprawled out in an odd position and she was wearing what appeared to be a red bathrobe. There was a cell phone not far from her right hand, as if the woman had dropped it during a fall.

Gloria sprang to her feet and fumbled inside her purse for her cell phone. Her fingers trembled as she dialed 911.

"Yes. This is Gloria Rutherford-Kennedy. I'm at 117 Eldridge Street in Belhaven. There's a woman lying face down in the basement and she's cold to the touch."

The operator's voice remained calm as she repeated the address and informed Gloria an ambulance and squad car had been dispatched. "Do you want me to stay on the line with you?"

"Yes. Please. At least until I'm outside. Gloria led Mally up the steps, to the car and coaxed her inside. "I'm outside, near my car." She thanked the 911 operator and began pacing the side yard when she noticed the shed door was ajar. She wiggled her foot back and forth, gently nudging the door open.

Several unopened boxes lined the small workbench. A twist tiller was propped in one corner and a shovel hung on a hook near the door. Gloria pulled her cell phone from her purse and snapped a picture of the inside before making her way to a window on the back of the house.

She bounced up on her tiptoes and peered inside the tidy kitchen. The light over the stove was on. Her eyes traveled along the counter, taking in the empty coffee pot and noting a frozen dinner container on the kitchen counter.

The faint sound of sirens echoed in the air. Gloria hurriedly snapped a couple more pictures before slipping the phone into her purse.

A police car roared around the corner and stopped in front of the house. Moments later, an ambulance pulled in behind the police car. The vehicle doors flew open and uniformed officers and paramedics met Gloria in the driveway.

"She's downstairs." Gloria led the group through the breezeway, down the steps and to the woman's body. After a brief explanation of how she found her, Gloria climbed the stairs and waited near the top.

"She's gone." The ambulance driver said as he passed Gloria. He returned moments later, carrying a stretcher.

A female officer, who looked vaguely familiar, stepped into the breezeway and approached

Gloria. "You're the one who found the deceased?"

"Yes. I stopped by this afternoon to drop off some vegetables and my homemade rhubarb pie, kind of a 'welcome to the neighborhood' gesture." Gloria proceeded to tell the officer how she rang the front doorbell before going around back. "No one answered, so I opened the breezeway door to set the stuff inside and my springer spaniel, Mally, snuck past me and ran into the house. I tried to get her to come out, but when she didn't, I went in after her. That's when I found the woman's body. Is it the property owner, Ms. Hines?"

"We're still working on identifying the deceased." The officer reached inside her pocket and pulled out a pen and pad of paper. "You look familiar. Didn't I meet you at an old farmhouse not long ago where the new property owner found a body inside?"

Gloria studied the officer's face. "Yes. I remember you. My friend, Lucy Carlson, purchased a home to renovate and when my friends and I went to take a look at it, we found a man's body in the bedroom upstairs."

"Ah." The woman nodded. "Officer Joe Nelson and I were the first on scene."

"You're right." Gloria snapped her fingers. "You're Officer Bowling."

"Bowman," the woman corrected. "Deputy Sheriff Elaine Bowman. Nelson had you pegged. I remember him telling me to take a good look at your face because I'd see you again." She smirked. "I guess I didn't realize it would be so soon."

Gloria frowned. "I do seem to be in the wrong place at the wrong time quite often. I can assure you I had nothing to do with this poor woman's demise."

"Say...you're married to Paul Kennedy."

"I'm his wife."

"I bet you met him while he was working, too."

Gloria's frown deepened.

Thankfully, another officer approached. "Hey Bow. We need you out here."

"Don't leave," Deputy Bowman told Gloria.

"I wouldn't dream of it," Gloria muttered under her breath, and then followed the woman outdoors. She started to make her way to the front porch when she spotted Mally vaulting over the car seat, so she opened the car door. "C'mon. Let's wait out front."

A layer of leaves crunched under Gloria's feet as she circled a large tree in the front yard before plopping down on the porch steps.

She watched as Mally sniffed a row of bushes before taking care of business. Several cars drove past, including Bea McQueen's MINI Cooper. Gloria knew it wouldn't be long before the entire

Town of Belhaven was cruising by...and Annabelle was in plain sight.

Gloria plucked her cell phone from her purse and dialed Paul's cell phone number. He didn't answer so she left a voice mail, telling him to call her as soon as possible.

Her next call was to Lucy, who also didn't answer.

Gloria tried Dot's Restaurant but ended the call when she spotted Dot's dark blue van pull up out front. She hopped off the porch and darted to the van.

Dot rolled down the window. "I thought Bea was kidding when she ran into the restaurant telling everyone she spotted your car, along with several emergency vehicles, in front of Vanessa's place."

"Great. I'm sure the whole town knows," Gloria groaned.

Dot nodded to the street, lined with police cars. "It must be a slow day for the Montbay County Sheriff's Department."

"No kidding." Gloria briefly explained what had transpired, how Mally had snuck past her, into Vanessa's house and that she'd discovered a woman lying face down at the bottom of the stairs.

"That's terrible," Dot said. "I guess you never know when it's your turn. It has to be Vanessa Hines. From what I've heard, she's pretty young, too young to have a heart attack."

"I don't know. I couldn't hear what the investigators were saying."

Deputy Bowman approached the side of the van. "You're free to leave. I have your statement but I'm sure we'll have more questions." She asked Gloria for her cell phone and home phone numbers and then disappeared around the side of the house.

"I better get out of here before they change their minds," Gloria said.

"Are you gonna stop by the restaurant?" Dot asked. "All the girls are there, waiting to find out what happened."

"Yeah. I left a voice mail for Paul but he hasn't called me back yet. I'll be there in a minute."

Dot sped off while Mally and Gloria headed to her car.

Gloria circled Main Street twice before she found an empty parking spot. She made her way to the employee break area in the back where she looped Mally's leash around a picnic table leg. "I won't be long," she promised.

She walked to the front of the building and stepped inside the restaurant. A heat crept up Gloria's neck as the room grew quiet and she felt the curious stares of the diners.

"Over here," Margaret hollered and Gloria hurried to the table in the back.

Ruth pulled out a chair and patted the seat. "Welcome to the party."

"Thanks." Gloria slid onto the seat. "I can't believe what just happened. The police haven't confirmed it, but I think I found Vanessa Hines' body. Talk about being in the wrong place at the wrong time."

"You certainly have a knack for finding bodies," Ruth said.

Gloria laid out the series of events leading up to the discovery of the woman's body.

"Good heavens," Rose said. "I do believe I'm gonna have to whip up a special potion to protect you from harm."

"Or everyone around her," Andrea joked.

"Ain't that the truth." Gloria caught a glimpse of Lucy's red head as she scurried to the table. "I got here as fast as I could."

Rose moved her chair closer to Dot to make room for Lucy.

"What did I miss?"

"We think Vanessa Hines is dead. Gloria found her body and we're not sure if the cause of death was foul play."

"What did the inside of her place look like?" Margaret asked.

"Was it trashed?" Andrea asked.

"I didn't go in the house," Gloria said. "I made it as far as the breezeway and the basement."

"But?" Lucy prompted.

"But what?"

Dot shook her head. "You're telling us you found a woman's body, called 911 and then waited for the police to arrive without taking a look around."

"I did take a quick peek in the windows on the back side of the house before the police arrived. I also looked inside the shed. Both were clean. Maybe she had a heart attack. I mean, moving is stressful."

"So nothing looked out of place?" Lucy asked.

"See for yourself." Gloria pulled her cell phone from her purse, switched it on, scrolled to a picture of Vanessa's kitchen and handed the phone to Lucy.

Lucy's eyes squinted. "It looks like there's a frozen dinner on the counter." She handed the phone to Margaret.

"There's no coffee in the pot." Margaret handed the phone to Andrea.

"Check out the bouquet of flowers on the table," Andrea said.

"Flowers?" Gloria took the phone from Andrea and studied the picture. Sure enough, there was a large bouquet of festive fall flowers in the center of the table. "Maybe it was a housewarming gift."

"Or a clue," Dot said. "Let me see."

Gloria handed the phone to Dot. "Yeah. They look fresh, like she just got them," Dot said before handing the phone back.

"At least I have an alibi. I was in church all morning and with Paul until I left to visit the shut-ins. The Fords can vouch for me and so can Al Dickerson, plus I left a note on Stan McTavish's door."

"There's something else." Ruth shifted uneasily. "I was gonna call you last night. Bea was in the post office yesterday. She said she stopped by to welcome Vanessa to Belhaven and mentioned one of the Garden Girls would be stopping by to welcome her to the area."

"We do that for everyone," Dot pointed out.

"True. When Vanessa found out Gloria was one of the Garden Girls, she said she would welcome all of us into her house. Everyone that is, except for Gloria."

Chapter 3

Gloria's jaw dropped. "Because she has a crush on my husband? That's not my fault." Looking back now, she wished she had taken Ruth or Dot up on their offer to let them visit the woman.

"I hate to say this, but I hope the woman died of natural causes," Andrea said quietly.

"I'm sure Bea, the blabbermouth, is burning up the phone lines; telling everyone Vanessa didn't want Gloria to come to her house and the next thing you know, Vanessa is dead and Gloria is the one who found her body," Ruth said.

"We don't know for sure the dead woman is Vanessa." Gloria's phone beeped. She snatched it off the table and flipped it over. "It's Paul. I'm going to step outside." She headed for the back door, anxious to avoid the diners' curious stares.

"Hi Paul."

"Hi dear. Sorry I missed your call earlier. I was in the barn, replacing some of the loft floorboards. The place is starting to shape up nicely. I have some ideas for lighting. I'll show you when you get home."

"Great. I can hardly wait to hear them."

"Have you finished visiting the shut-ins?" Paul asked.

"Sort of." Gloria sucked in a breath. "Vanessa Hines was on my list of people to visit. When I got to her house, no one answered so I opened the breezeway door to leave a pie and bag of vegetables for her. Mally managed to sneak past me, into the house and when she wouldn't come out, I had to go get here. That's when I found a woman sprawled out at the bottom of the stairs."

"Is she all right?"

"She's not. She's...dead."

"You said you stopped to visit Vanessa Hines. I know a Vanessa Hines. She works for the county fire department."

"I believe she's the same woman, but again, the police haven't confirmed her identity. If the woman is Vanessa Hines, she told several people she didn't want me at her house. She had a thing for you."

There was a long silence on the other end.

"Paul?"

"Vanessa worked for the county for a few years. I had no idea she was after me."

"I didn't either, not until the girls told me earlier this week," Gloria said. "From what I heard, she moved to Belhaven to be close to you."

"You knew that and yet you still stopped by her house to welcome her?"

"I figured the rumor wasn't true and it was just a bunch of gossip."

"I'm sure you were shocked to find her body," Paul said.

"I'm thinking she may have died of natural causes." *Face down at the bottom of her stairs,* Gloria silently added.

"Let me make a few phone calls to see what I can find out," Paul said. "Where are you?"

"At Dot's Restaurant. I'll be home shortly." Gloria told her husband good-bye and then disconnected the line before stepping back inside the restaurant and joining her friends.

"Paul is going to try to confirm the woman's identity," Gloria said in a low voice.

Rose patted Gloria's hand. "I'm sure the authorities will get to the bottom of this."

"I better get going." Gloria promised she would call her friends as soon as she found anything else out and then stopped by to grab Mally before heading home.

When they reached the farm, Mally made a beeline for the barn.

Gloria placed her purse and keys on top of the car before following her pooch.

The smell of fresh sawdust, mingled with the sweet smell of hay bales lingered in the air.

It took a second for her eyes to adjust to the barn's shadowy interior and she caught a glimpse of Paul inside the milking parlor. "I'm home."

Paul wandered to the doorway and pulled his wife into his arms. "I'm glad you're safe."

Gloria placed her cheek against Paul's chest and closed her eyes. "I feel terrible for the poor woman." She took a step back. "Did you call the station?"

"Yes. The woman you found was Vanessa Hines. It's too early for the investigators to rule on the cause of death, but the medical staff on scene suspect it was some sort of head injury," Paul said. "I've seen those types of injuries before. It's possible she lost her balance and tumbled down the steps, hitting her head."

"So it could be accidental," Gloria said.

"Yes, although there was also a bruise forming on the side of her forehead, which may have been caused by blunt force trauma."

"Meaning someone struck her."

"Yes." Paul shifted his feet. "There's something else."

Gloria could tell from the tone of his voice she wasn't going to like what he was about to say.

"Vanessa's cell phone was found near her body."

Gloria nodded. "I noticed it near her right hand. Of course, I didn't touch anything and called the police."

"I wasn't supposed to hear this, but the last number Vanessa called was your cell phone."

"Mine?" The blood drained from Gloria's face. "I never talked to her. Let me check my phone." She jogged to the car, grabbed her purse, pulled her cell phone out and returned to the barn.

She turned the phone on and scrolled through the recent log of phone numbers. There was one call, an unknown number, at 6:47 p.m. the previous evening. "I don't know who this is." Gloria handed the phone to her husband.

Paul shifted his gaze and stared at the screen. "I don't recognize the number either and I don't dare call it. It's a local number."

"Paul," Gloria whispered. "Ruth told me that Vanessa didn't want me in her house. What if Vanessa called to tell me not to come over? I never took the call. Can I see my phone for a minute?"

Paul handed his wife the phone and she dialed Ruth's number.

"Hi Gloria."

"Hi Ruth. I have a quick question. Remember when you told me Vanessa didn't want me to come to her place? I'm wondering if someone gave her my cell phone number."

Gloria paused. "I see. Thanks. I gotta go." She disconnected the line before Ruth could ask questions. "Bea McQueen gave Vanessa my cell phone number."

She began to pace. "She must've tried to call to tell me not to come over but I didn't take the call. This looks so bad."

"Try not to worry," Paul said. "We still don't know the official cause of death."

Despite Paul's assurance Gloria shouldn't worry, she was deeply concerned. Several locals knew Vanessa had a thing for Paul. What kind of person would move to be close to a man they knew was married?

Vanessa told Bea she didn't want Gloria in her house. To top it all off, Gloria's number was the last one Vanessa had called and Gloria was the one who found her body. "I'm going to head inside."

"I'll wrap things up here," Paul said.

When she reached the house, Gloria dropped her purse on the table and hung her keys on the hook near the door.

She wandered aimlessly from room to room, praying the poor woman's death was accidental or from natural causes. Maybe Vanessa had lost her footing and tumbled down the stairs.

A sudden thought occurred to Gloria. What if Vanessa had moved to get away from someone and that someone had tracked her down and murdered her? Paul had mentioned bruising near her forehead.

To take her mind off Vanessa's death, Gloria decided to whip up a batch of "breakfast bombs" for dinner.

She grabbed a tube of biscuit dough from the fridge, along with butter, eggs, milk, cheese and a packet of bacon bits.

Gloria preheated the oven and then whisked some whole milk and eggs before pouring the mixture into a heated skillet. She scrambled the eggs, removed the pan from the heat and sprinkled some chives on top.

Next, she flattened each biscuit round on a greased baking sheet and then topped each round with a scoop of scrambled eggs. She sprinkled bacon and cheese on top of the eggs before pinching the edges of the dough together.

Gloria carefully flipped the dough balls so that they were seam side down before sliding the baking sheet into the pre-heated oven.

After the breakfast bombs finished baking, Gloria removed the pan from the oven and shut it off. She brushed the tops of each breakfast bomb with melted butter and sprinkled poppy seeds on top.

"Perfect." Gloria slid the pan to the back of the stove and then removed her apron.

Mally and Puddles, Gloria's cat, watched her work and when she finished, she gave each of them a treat before grabbing her sweater and wandering out onto the porch.

Fall was in full swing and after a huge windstorm the previous week, most of the trees' leaves had fallen to the ground and were begging to be raked.

Gloria's grandsons, Ryan and Tyler, planned to come over to help her rake and work on some small projects in the barn with Paul.

A blast of cold air ruffled Gloria's hair and she wrapped her sweater tighter as she rocked back and forth.

The whole town of Belhaven probably knew Vanessa had moved to the area to be close to Paul. It was an unfortunate series of events, but Gloria knew there was no way the authorities could seriously consider her as a suspect.

No. The woman must have whacked her head on something, not realized the severity of her injury and suffered a fatal hemorrhage.

The sight of a bright pink Cadillac racing past the house caught Gloria's attention. It was followed by the sound of tires squealing. The Cadillac reappeared as it backed up and then careened into the driveway before screeching to a halt near the bottom of the porch steps.

A plume of dust filled the air. Gloria waved her hand in front of her face and watched as Eleanor Whittaker climbed out of the car and strolled to the porch.

"Hi Eleanor."

"Hi Gloria. I was on my way to Evelyn Christensen's house to play bridge when I saw you sitting on the porch and thought I'd stop by for a minute."

"I see you're getting around now that you took your car out of storage," Gloria said. "Are you sure you're ready to drive?"

"I'm fit as a fiddle," Eleanor insisted. "Why, I've been all over the place, to Green Springs and Rockville. This morning, I drove to church. I saw you sitting near the front, but you know how busy the Sunday service is, so I didn't get a chance to say hello."

"Would you like to join me?" Gloria patted the empty rocker next to her.

"Sure." Eleanor glanced at her watch. "I have a few minutes before the bridge game starts." She climbed the porch steps and settled into the empty seat. "I wanted to let you know there's no way I think you had anything to do with Vanessa Hines' murder."

"We don't know that she was murdered," Gloria said. "But thank you."

"Well, I was down at the Quik Stop to pick up some root beer and peanuts to take to the bridge game and Sally Keane was working. She said Joe, you know, Officer Joe Nelson and she are still an item."

"I had no idea," Gloria said. "Poor Joe."

Sally Keane was the community complainer. She complained about her job. She complained about living in a small town. She complained about the weather. The summers were too hot. Fall was too windy and winters were too cold.

Gloria tried to avoid shopping at the Quik Stop if she knew Sally was working.

"Well, Joe said it looked like someone attacked Vanessa and then pushed her down the stairs. Course I promised to keep mum about it, but I felt that since you were involved, you'd want to know."

"I appreciate it," Gloria said. "Let me guess, Bea McQueen is spreading the rumor that Vanessa didn't want me at her house."

Eleanor averted her gaze and stared at her hands in her lap.

"I had hoped the woman's death was accidental, but Sally Keane's inside scoops are usually spot on." *Unfortunately, this put Gloria right in the hot seat.*

"I best get going." Eleanor slid out of the chair. "There's one more thing and I almost hesitate to mention it."

Gloria tilted her head. "What is it?" she asked softly, but already had a sneaking suspicion it had to do with Vanessa's death.

"There was a vase of flowers on Vanessa's kitchen table."

"You're right. There were," Gloria said.

"There was a card with the flowers and the card had Paul's name on it."

Chapter 4

"I'm sorry Gloria," Eleanor hurriedly continued. "I shouldn't have said anything but I figured you would find out."

"I...it's okay, Eleanor. I appreciate you giving me a heads up."

"From what I've heard, the woman was a little off, so I wouldn't be surprised if she sent the flowers to herself." Eleanor patted Gloria's arm. "I better go. If I'm late, the girls are going to make me throw an extra five in the kitty."

Eleanor hurried to her car and hopped in. She revved up the engine before spinning her tires and disappearing in the same cloud of dust in which she'd arrived.

Gloria stared blankly at the empty driveway and then shifted her gaze to the open barn doors.

The small, awful thought that maybe something had been going on between Vanessa and Paul crept into her mind. What if the rumor was true?

She slowly closed her eyes and leaned her head against the back of the rocker. It didn't make sense for a grown woman to move to a small town, where she knew very few people and then go around telling everyone she moved to be close to a man...a married man who was decades older.

Paul and Gloria hadn't been married long. Did he regret marrying her? What if all those times he told her he'd taken on part-time jobs, he had been rendezvousing with Vanessa?

A knot formed in the pit of Gloria's stomach and she began to feel nauseous. If it were true, her world would crumble around her. She loved Paul with all of her heart. She trusted him implicitly and knew he trusted her.

What if it was her fault? Had Gloria's constant sleuthing driven her husband into the arms of another woman?

Surely, Paul would hear about the flowers and card. He knew Gloria was making her rounds to visit the newcomers and shut-ins. Maybe he wasn't aware that she planned to stop by Vanessa's place to welcome her to Belhaven. He'd said as much when Gloria first told him about Vanessa's body.

Gloria pushed the thoughts from her mind and headed inside to finish their breakfast/dinner. During dinner, she forced herself to carry on a light conversation but her voice sounded wooden and hollow. Her sentences were short and choppy.

"The breakfast bombs are delicious." Paul reached for his third.

"Thanks. The kids loved these growing up," Gloria said. "You can use bacon, like I did, or ham, which is just as good."

Gloria went through the motions as she cleaned the dishes and put the leftovers in the fridge. If Paul knew about the flowers, if he sent them to Vanessa, he was doing an excellent job of hiding it from his wife.

Paul helped his wife clean up the kitchen and then Gloria hung the damp kitchen towel on the front of the stove. "I'm going to turn in early."

She avoided his gaze as she hurried out of the kitchen. After brushing her teeth and washing her face, she climbed into bed and curled up into a ball, tucking the covers under her chin. She tried to pray, to pour her heart out to God, but it came out as a jumbled mess, and she finally gave up.

A short time later, Paul crept into bed. He lay there quietly for a few moments and she knew he was trying to figure out if she were still awake but Gloria never moved so Paul finally rolled over and soon, his soft snores filled the dark room.

It was early morning before Gloria finally fell into a fitful sleep and she woke early. Paul was still sleeping when Mally and she made their way to the kitchen for their morning ritual of coffee and bathroom breaks.

Her cell phone was still in her purse, and the battery was low; so she plugged it into the charger and scrolled through the screen. She'd missed several phone calls from the previous evening. There was one from Dot, Margaret, Lucy, Ruth and Andrea. There were even calls from Rose and Alice.

"They know," Gloria whispered. "They heard the rumor."

It was still early when Paul shuffled into the kitchen. "You didn't sleep well, either."

"No." Gloria smoothed her hair and wondered if Paul still found her attractive.

He poured a cup of coffee, eased into the chair across from her and squeezed his wife's hand. "Don't worry, dear. It will be all right. I'm sure the authorities will figure out what happened. We both know you didn't murder Vanessa."

Gloria's first instinct was to snatch her hand away, but she knew it was childish and Paul would be confused. Instead, she slid off her chair and scooched onto his lap, snuggling against him.

Paul wrapped his arms around her. "We'll get through this. I know you're concerned. I'd be lying if I said I wasn't concerned, but it will be fine."

"Yes, it will," Gloria whispered into his neck. She lifted her head and smiled. "Why don't I fix us some leftovers?"

She forced her nagging suspicions from her mind, and they ate the leftover breakfast bombs with a side of mixed fruit and wheat toast. After eating, Paul headed to the barn to continue working on the repairs while Gloria cleaned up.

She'd finished loading the dishwasher and rinsing out the coffee pot when she spotted a police car pulling into the drive.

Gloria wandered out onto the porch and waited until Deputy Bowman reached the bottom step. "Hello Mrs. Kennedy."

"Hello Deputy Bowman."

"I'm sorry to bother you this early but wondered if I might ask you a few more questions."

"Of course." Gloria motioned her inside. "Would you like a cup of coffee?"

"No ma'am. Detective Jack Green is meeting me here. He should be here at any moment."

"I see." The women chatted about the weather until a four-door sedan with tinted windows pulled into the drive and parked next to the patrol car. The vehicle was identical to the one Paul drove when he was still part of the police force.

The man exited the vehicle and made his way to the porch. "Hello Deputy Bowman." He nodded to Gloria. "I take it Deputy Bowman has explained that we would like to ask you a few more questions."

"Yes." Gloria held the door open for the officers. "Please come in." She stepped inside as Paul trudged across the driveway and joined them in the kitchen where he nodded to the deputy and Detective Green.

"Jack. Haven't seen you in a while." Paul and the detective shook hands.

"Good to see you, Paul. I wish it was under better circumstances," Detective Green said. "I'm here to ask a few questions about Ms. Hines' death."

"Of course." Paul nodded and settled into the seat near the door. "We have nothing to hide."

Deputy Bowman spoke first, asking Gloria to recount the events leading up to finding Vanessa's body at the bottom of the stairs. She repeated the story. "Have the examiners determined the cause of death?"

"Blunt force trauma, which triggered an undetected aneurysm," Detective Green replied. "It could have been caused by being struck or taking a hard fall, such as falling to the bottom of the stairs. It appears the incident may have occurred up to 24 hours prior to Ms. Hines' demise, so we're questioning others who may have been in contact with her to try to retrace her steps."

Gloria let out the breath she'd been holding. "Which means she could have been lying at the bottom of her stairs for some time."

"Yes. It's possible. Unfortunately, your number was the last number Ms. Hines called before her death, and her cell phone was found near her body."

"That doesn't make my wife a killer," Paul said.

"Of course not. As I said, we're following up on all leads." Deputy Bowman turned to Paul. "I'm glad you're here as well, Mr. Kennedy. I have a couple questions for you."

"Okay," Paul replied evenly. "I'm not sure how I can assist you in your investigation."

Deputy Bowman flipped through her notepad. "During our search of Ms. Hines' house, we found a bouquet of fresh flowers on her kitchen table..." Her voice trailed off.

Detective Green cleared his throat. "There was a card attached to the bouquet and your name was on the card."

"What?" Paul roared. "I've never sent Vanessa Hines flowers in my life."

Deputy Bowman asked Paul to recount his whereabouts for the past several days.

He told her his entire schedule from Friday morning through Sunday afternoon, when Gloria called 911 and reported finding Vanessa's body.

"Thank you for your time." Detective Green's chair scraped loudly against the linoleum as he pushed it back. "Again, this is only a preliminary investigation. We haven't named either of you as suspects, merely persons of interest due to your involvement with the victim."

The home phone began to ring. "If you'll excuse me," Paul said, and made his way over to the phone.

Deputy Bowman and Detective Green stepped onto the porch and Gloria followed them out. "You'll keep us posted?"

"Of course, Mrs. Kennedy." Detective Green nodded his head and strode to his car.

The women watched Green climb inside his vehicle and pull out onto the road.

"I'm sorry you have to go through this," Deputy Bowman said. "I knew Ms. Hines personally since she was a clerk at the Montbay County Fire Department." She lowered her voice. "She had more enemies than friends."

The words hung in the air as Deputy Bowman tipped her hat and climbed into her patrol car before backing out of the driveway and speeding off.

Now all Gloria had to do was figure out who those enemies were.

Chapter 5

Gloria walked back inside the house, pulling the door closed behind her.

Paul leaned his back against the counter and crossed his arms. "I wondered why you were so quiet last night. I chalked it up to the shock of finding Vanessa's body." He shifted slightly and met her gaze. "You knew about the card and the flowers."

"I did," Gloria confessed. "And I'm ashamed to say the thought crept into my mind that you did send them to her."

"That something was going on between us," Paul pressed.

"Yes." Gloria whispered. "But the more I thought about it, I knew it wasn't true."

Paul stared at his wife before he stepped away from the counter. He walked past Gloria and wordlessly exited the kitchen, quietly closing the door behind him.

Gloria dropped her head into her hands and began to cry.

She sobbed for several long moments and Mally began to whine. Gloria patted her pup's head. "I'm such an idiot."

Her shoulder's shook as she sobbed. Finally, she lifted her head. *Pull yourself together.*

Gloria sucked in a deep breath and headed to the bathroom where she threw on a pair of sweatpants and a sweater before grabbing her purse and heading outdoors.

The barn door was closed and Paul's car was gone. Gloria slowly made her way to the garage. She eased Annabelle out of the garage, steered the car out onto the road and drove toward town.

Dot's was packed, so Gloria coasted past the restaurant, circled the block and inched along a narrow back alley, parking behind the post office where her car was out of sight.

She slipped out of the car and tiptoed to the open back door of the post office, cupping her hands to her eyes as she peered inside the building. "Hello?"

Kenny Webber, the rural route carrier, made his way to the door. "Hi Gloria. Ruth figured you might pop in." He swung the door open and Gloria stepped into the back of the post office.

Through the glass panels of the mailboxes, Gloria could see several people standing in the lobby, so she slipped behind a rack of postal supplies.

Finally, Ruth caught Gloria's eye and hurried over. "Good heavens almighty. You got this whole town in an uproar. Both you and Paul. I heard the police were on your doorstep this morning. What happened?"

Ruth leaned in and studied Gloria's face. "Have you been crying? Don't tell me you bought into the crap that Paul bought those flowers for Vanessa. It was a setup." She twirled her finger next to her forehead. "I heard the lady was crazier than a loon."

"I don't think Paul sent her flowers," Gloria said. "I mean, the thought did cross my mind last night after Eleanor stopped by to tell me the vase of flowers on Vanessa's table had a card with Paul's name on it."

"I heard the woman had a bunch of enemies. I think someone is trying to frame you," Ruth said.

"No kidding. It doesn't help that she told people she was after Paul and she didn't want me at her house. I found her body and her flowers had Paul's name on them," Gloria's shoulders sagged. "The final nail in the coffin was the fact that Vanessa's cell phone was found near her body and the last number she called was mine. They might as well put the cuffs on now."

"What does Paul say about all of this?" Ruth asked.

Gloria closed her eyes. "I don't know. We're not talking to each other."

"Oh good grief. Wait here." Ruth tromped over to the other side of the post office. "Kenny, we got a 911 emergency. Can you cover for about half an hour while we run over to Dot's place?"

"Sure. Take your time."

Ruth grabbed Gloria's arm and led her through the back door. "We can't drive your car. Let's take the mail truck."

"Not the mail truck."

"It's our only option," Ruth said. "Crawl to the other side and lay low."

Gloria obeyed Ruth's orders and crawled to the back of the truck, squeezing in between two tall towers of shipping boxes.

Ruth climbed into the driver's seat and flipped the ignition before shifting into gear. "Hang on."

They bumped down the alley and drove for several minutes. After several more jarring bumps, Ruth shifted into park. "We're here."

Gloria crawled out of the mail truck and grinned when she realized Ruth had driven behind the Main Street buildings and parked near Dot's employee area in the back.

"You wait here and I'll go round up the others." Ruth hurried into the restaurant's kitchen area while Gloria perched on the picnic table bench.

In less than 24 hours, she'd gone from a happy-go-lucky newlywed, to a woman being questioned for murder and her husband was under suspicion for his involvement with the deceased.

Paul and Gloria rarely fought. He'd never walked out like he had that morning. She prayed they could recover from the crisis.

The back door to the restaurant flew open and Ruth, followed by Dot, Rose, Margaret, Lucy and Andrea, poured out.

Alice joined the group moments later. "Oh Miss Gloria. We are so sorry. This is terrible."

"It's worse than terrible. May I?" Ruth asked Gloria.

Gloria waved her hand in defeat. "Be my guest. Tell them everything."

The girls huddled around the table as Ruth shared the news of the flowers, followed by the visit from Detective Green and Deputy Bowman, how the woman's last phone call had been to Gloria.

"You don't believe Paul was having a fling with this woman, do you?" Margaret asked.

"I. No. I mean, last night when Eleanor stopped by to tell me, I was shocked and a small thought ran through my head, but by this morning I knew it wasn't true," Gloria said.

"What does Paul say?" Lucy asked.

"We're not talking. After the investigators left, he asked me if I believed it. I admitted that the thought had crossed my mind but I knew it wasn't true. He left the house, and I don't know where he went." Gloria folded her arms, placed her head on top, praying it was all a bad dream, and at any moment, she would wake up.

"Oh dear," Rose said. "Once this all blows over, I have the perfect love potion to reunite you."

"*I* have the love potions," Alice insisted. "Stick to your fountain of youth stuff."

"Ladies." Dot lifted her hand. "By the time this is over, Gloria might need both. But for now, we need to figure out how to clear Gloria's name and somehow prove Paul wasn't involved with Vanessa Hines."

Gloria lifted her head. "After Detective Jack Green left, Deputy Bowman told me Vanessa Hines had more enemies than friends."

"So now we have to figure out who those enemies were, someone who had it in for Vanessa and hated her so much they may have killed her," Andrea said.

"Piece of cake," Lucy said.

"Right," Dot said. "The sooner, the better so we can get the lovebirds reunited."

Ruth stood. "I gotta get back to the post office. Kenny needs to start his morning route. Why don't you let me start digging around? I've got a few friends with connections to the fire department."

"We'll keep our eyes and ears open here at the restaurant," Rose said. "Vanessa's murder is the talk of the town, so I'm sure someone will be able to shed a little more light on Ms. Hines' recent activities."

"Thanks everyone," Gloria said. "I can't believe this is happening. Maybe by the time I get home, Paul will be there, and we can sit down and discuss this rationally."

Gloria thanked her friends again before climbing back into the mail truck. Ruth followed behind.

When they reached the post office's rear parking lot, Ruth pulled into an empty spot and turned to face Gloria. "I know how much you love a good mystery, my friend, but you may be a little too close to this for you to remain objective."

"So you're telling me to cool my jets," Gloria said.

"Yes. In other words, hang tight, stay out of sight and let the rest of us girls spearhead an investigation for a change."

"Thanks Ruth." Gloria's eyes filled with tears as she hugged her friend. "I feel like I'm living my worst nightmare. Do you think Paul will forgive me for doubting him?"

"He's a smart man," Ruth said. "He'll forgive you and if he doesn't, we'll knock some sense into him."

Gloria hopped out of the mail truck and brushed the dirt from her sweatpants. "I have the best friends in the world. I don't know what I would do without you, without all of you."

"The feeling is mutual," Ruth said. "You have saved every single one of our hides at one time or another. Now it's time for us to return the favor."

Chapter 6

When Gloria arrived home, Paul's car was still gone so she sent him a text with only two words... "I'm sorry."

She tried to take her mind off her worries by playing a computer game but couldn't focus. Gloria gave up and decided she needed to get out of the house, so she grabbed a light sweater and Mally, and they headed to the back of the property.

Mally knew where they were going as she ran ahead and waited for Gloria near the edge of the woods. During the summer months, the creek had filled, almost overflowing the banks, but October had been a dry month and the water line finally receded.

When Gloria caught up, her pooch tromped to the edge of the creek before taking a drink and then trotted deeper into the woods to investigate a squirrel who scampered up a nearby pine tree.

Gloria sat on the edge of a broken tree trunk and mindlessly watched Mally. She knew in her heart Paul hadn't given Vanessa Hines the flowers. She trusted her husband implicitly. But if he hadn't, who had? The killer?

Detective Green mentioned Vanessa might have sustained a blow to her head up to 24 hours prior to her death. Had she argued with someone inside her home? Maybe she hit her head and recovered, thinking she was all right. Or perhaps she lost her footing near the top of her basement steps and tumbled to the bottom.

The woman had worked for the Montbay County Fire Department. Perhaps it was a co-worker.

Gloria didn't personally know any of the fire department staff. Paul did, which was how he knew Vanessa. The local sheriff department and fire department often worked hand in hand.

She knew Pearl Johnson was a dispatcher at the sheriff's department. There was also Minnie Dexter, Judith Arnett's cousin. Minnie had given Gloria some useful information during an investigation at the police department right around the time Paul and Gloria wed.

Minnie was a busybody, a lot like her cousin, Judith. And although Judith, a Belhaven local, and Gloria weren't the best of friends, they had reached a sort of truce over the last couple of years. In fact, Judith, via Ruth, had been instrumental in setting up a meeting between Gloria and Minnie so she could glean some clues in the previous case.

Gloria wondered if perhaps she could chat with Minnie again. Ruth and Judith were friends. She abruptly sprang from the log. "C'mon Mally. We can't sit around waiting to see what happens." Despite Ruth's advice to step aside and allow the other Garden Girls do a little investigating into Vanessa's death, she couldn't just sit back and do nothing.

When they reached the house, Gloria led Mally inside and began working on whipping up a quick lunch, in case Paul came back, and he was hungry.

After making some sandwiches and placing them in the fridge, Gloria texted Ruth, asking her to call when she was on her lunch break.

Paul's daughter, Allison, or Allie, had recently been hired as a dispatcher at the Montbay County Sheriff's Department and Gloria briefly thought about calling her, but quickly decided against dragging Paul's daughter into the middle of their mess.

No, Minnie was her best bet.

Ruth called at twelve on the dot. "What's up?"

"I was wondering if Judith Arnett has been in the post office today."

"Yes, her and every other Belhaven resident," Ruth ranted. "Word on the street is Vanessa was on the verge of being fired from the fire department."

Gloria perked up. "Oh really?"

"Yeah. Something about she filed harassment claims against a couple of her co-workers and she was also being investigated for leaving the station during working hours while she was on the clock."

"What does Judith say?"

"That her cousin, Minnie, claims to have the scoop on the parties involved."

"Perfect," Gloria said. "Do you think you could set up a meeting with Minnie, Judith, you and me so we can talk to her?"

"I thought you were going to let me and the others work on this," Ruth said. "Never mind. I should've known that wasn't gonna happen. Let me see what I can put together. When do you want to meet?"

"As soon as possible. Thanks Ruth."

"You're welcome. I gotta go so I can eat something while Kenny handles the madhouse out front. One more thing. You know Minnie's deal so you'll have to bring some goodies."

"Goodies?" Gloria asked.

"I'm guessing food. Probably pizzas."

"Oh, I forgot." The last time they'd asked for Minnie's help, it had involved pizza and breadsticks, a whole meat lover's pizza to be exact...for Minnie. "Pizza it is. Whatever she wants."

Gloria thanked Ruth again for working on arranging a meeting before hanging up. She wondered if the local news had picked up the story of the harassment claims and headed to the computer in the dining room.

After settling in, Gloria's cat, Puddles, hopped onto her lap and nudged her hand. Gloria absentmindedly petted Puddles while she waited for the computer to warm up.

She wondered about Vanessa's co-workers, the ones she'd filed charges against and if they were married. What if one of them had decided to stop her, no matter what?

Several area residents knew Vanessa was enamored with Paul, enough to move to Belhaven. Surely, the workers at the fire department knew it, as well. Had one of them attempted to set Paul up and an unsuspecting Gloria, who was trying to do a good deed and welcome her to the neighborhood, had walked into a trap?

What if Vanessa filed sexual harassment claims and one or more of the firefighters were married and the spouses went to Vanessa's home to confront her? Jealously was a strong emotion. Or perhaps Vanessa and one of her co-workers became involved in a physical altercation.

Gloria checked her emails before searching the internet. She couldn't find any information on the harassment allegations and wondered if the

Montbay County Fire Department was keeping a tight lid on the allegations, making sure the local news didn't pick up the story.

Vanessa had died under suspicious circumstances and half the Town of Belhaven knew about the harassment claims. There was no way the fire department could keep it under wraps. If someone leaked the information to the press, it would help Gloria by widening the list of suspects.

There was still the issue of the flowers with Paul's name on them. Gloria was certain Paul was down at the sheriff's department trying to talk to former co-workers who may have known Vanessa.

Gloria's heart ached and she was deeply disappointed in herself for suspecting her loving husband of being attracted to another woman.

She logged off the computer and checked her cell phone to see if Paul replied, but there was nothing. *Please forgive me,* she whispered.

Her stomach started to grumble so Gloria took one of the sandwiches from the fridge, poured a glass of lemonade and slid into a kitchen chair before reaching for her Bible.

Gloria slipped her reading glasses on and opened the book to where she'd left off.

"Wherefore seeing we also are compassed about with so great a cloud of witnesses, let us lay aside every weight, and the sin which doth so easily beset us, and let us run with patience the race that is set before us,

Looking unto Jesus the author and finisher of our faith; who for the joy that was set before him endured the cross, despising the shame, and is set down at the right hand of the throne of God." Hebrews 12:1-2 (KJV)

They were powerful verses and Gloria swiped at a tear that trickled down her cheek. It was one of those moments she wished she could turn the clock back. She never would have gone to Vanessa Hines' house.

But there was no turning back. She was stuck in the middle of the mess and had to find a way out. She hoped Minnie could shed some light on Vanessa's recent past.

Paul texted a short time later, telling his wife he was "running some errands" and wouldn't be home until dinnertime. She thanked him for letting her know and began cleaning the house.

It had been almost a year since Paul and Gloria had married. The time had flown by and she was looking forward to the upcoming holidays and spending it with her children.

Paul and Gloria recently decided to visit Ben, Gloria's middle son, and his wife Kelly, who lived in the Houston area, in January. It would be a nice break from the winter doldrums and Allie had offered to stay at the farm to care for Mally and Puddles.

By the time 5:00 rolled around, the house was spotless and the floors clean enough to eat off, but she'd completely forgotten about dinner.

Her cell phone chirped and Ruth sent a cryptic message they were on for 5:30 and told her not to forget the "goods."

Gloria replied, asking her for a detailed list of the "goods" and then her phone rang.

"Are you okay with meeting Minnie at Judith's at 5:30? It's the only time Judith could fit us in. She joined Eleanor's Pilates class and it starts at six," a breathless Ruth said.

"Sure. I mean, Minnie is doing me - us - a favor so 5:30 will be fine. At Judith's place."

"At Judith's," Ruth confirmed.

"What kind of food should I bring? Should I order pizza again?" Gloria asked.

"Nope. No pizza. Minnie is on a diet. She's switched over to a more lucrative habit. Lottery tickets."

"Lottery tickets?"

"Yeah. The scratch-off kind," Ruth said. "Judith wasn't 100% certain which ones to buy so I would go with a variety pack."

Gloria wrinkled her nose. "I don't buy lottery tickets. Do you think I can get them at the Quik Stop?"

"Yeah. I've seen them in there. You might wanna get a move on. I would like to get to Judith's place before Minnie."

Gloria thanked Ruth and told her friend she was on the way. Paul hadn't arrived home yet so Gloria left a note on the table, telling him she was running an errand and that she would drop by Dot's Restaurant to pick up something for dinner before hurrying to the car.

When she reached downtown Belhaven, she found an empty parking spot near the corner grocery store and made her way inside.

Her heart sank when she spied Sally Keane. Sally was the last person she wanted to face right now but it was too late. She needed those scratch-offs.

Gloria made a beeline for the cash register, dropped her purse on the counter and reached for her wallet. "Hi Sally." She spotted a display case of lottery tickets on the wall behind Sally. "I need a few scratch-offs."

Sally lifted a brow. "A little hard up for cash these days?"

"No, they're not for me," Gloria said as she handed Sally a twenty-dollar bill. "Give me twenty dollars' worth and a variety."

Sally shifted to the side and began tearing scratch-off tickets from the roll. "The dollar tickets are junk. You might as well burn your money. Now, if you go with the five dollar tickets, you have a good chance of winning something."

"Fine. Give me some five dollar tickets." Gloria waved her hand.

"The Michigan lottery is up to ten million this week. You want to buy a Michigan Mega Millions?"

"How much is a ticket?"

"A dollar."

"Why not?" Gloria dug inside her change purse and pulled out four quarters. "I could use a little luck."

Sally took the money. "Odds of winning are like one in 258,000,000 but somebody has to win." She dropped the coins into the cash register. "I heard about Vanessa Hines. It's a shame about you finding her body and all. Course, I guess if anyone was going to find her body, it would be you."

"Right?" Gloria shoved the tickets in her purse and snapped it shut. "Rumor has it that Vanessa had her share of enemies. Maybe that's why she moved to Belhaven, to start over, get away from some bad blood."

"Well, she didn't move far enough away." Sally shivered. "She was in here Saturday afternoon, picking up some groceries and she told me she thought someone had followed her home from work Friday night."

Chapter 7

Gloria blinked rapidly. "She did? Did you tell Joe, I mean, Officer Nelson what she said?"

"Yep." Sally nodded. "Looking back, I wish I would've asked a few more questions about her suspicions, but you know me. I'm not one to pry into other people's business."

Gloria cleared her throat. "Yes, of course. We should always mind our own business."

"Anyhoo, Vanessa said she was freaked out about it. She said she wasn't able to get a good look at the vehicle because the bright lights were blinding her. She also mentioned she thought someone had been inside her house. She was on her way to Nails and Knobs to buy all new locks for her house."

Gloria's mind whirled. She had been the one to find Vanessa's body. There was no sign of forced entry, at least not that Gloria could see. Which meant, if there had been some sort of altercation inside her home, Vanessa had let the person or persons in.

"Thank you for the tickets, Sally." Gloria turned to go.

"Joe and I feel bad for you."

Gloria pivoted. "I guess I was in the wrong place at the wrong time."

"Yeah. That and the flowers. You live with someone, and you think you know them, but you don't."

Gloria clenched her fists, her fingernails digging into the palms of her hands. "I think it was a setup. Paul did *not* send Vanessa Hines flowers." She didn't wait for Sally to reply before marching out of the store and slamming the door behind her.

It was official. Everyone in Belhaven knew Vanessa Hines had a vase of flowers on her table with a card from Paul, except the flowers weren't from Paul.

She tossed her purse on the passenger seat and climbed behind the wheel. Gloria backed out onto the street and pressed the gas, a little too hard, causing her back tires to squeal as she burned rubber.

By the time she reached Judith's house, she'd calmed down. Of course the rumors were flying. She'd probably already been convicted of Vanessa's murder in the minds of some of the locals. Poor, jealous Gloria spotted the flowers while visiting Vanessa, and in a fit of rage, attacked the woman.

She parked on the side of the street and then made her way down the drive, past Ruth's van and Judith's car. She tapped lightly on the door before ringing the bell.

Ruth appeared in the doorway. "You look like you're ready to spit bullets."

"I just left the Quik Stop and Sally Keane was working."

Ruth rolled her eyes. "Ah. Enough said. The woman has the biggest mouth ever, not to mention she doesn't have an ounce of tact."

Gloria stepped into Judith's mudroom. Beyond the small mudroom was a large, open kitchen where Judith was seated at the table.

"Hello Gloria." Judith eased out of the chair and headed to the kitchen counter. "I made a fresh pot of coffee. Would you like a cup?"

"Yes please. Thank you for arranging a meeting with Minnie." She reached for the cup Judith held out and then took a small sip, eyeing the woman over the rim. "You look wonderful." Gloria pointed at her shimmering black workout pants and fitted blue blouse. "I adore your outfit."

"Thanks." Judith tugged on the top. "I love Eleanor's Pilates class. The woman has so much energy. I've started walking in the evenings, around the block, down Main Street and back around by the flea market. It's great exercise and has helped loosen my joints."

She went on. "I'm on the fence about trying Rose's energy elixir, although Eleanor swears by it."

"Side effects?" Gloria guessed.

"Yeah. I don't think I can handle the thought of cracking my knuckles every five minutes." She shrugged. "I can't stand the sound when Carl's knees crack after he gets up out of a chair."

Ruth chuckled. "Cracking your knuckles?"

"Yeah. Eleanor says she's gotten used to it but I think I'll take a pass since I'm thrilled with the way I'm feeling now."

A light rap on the back door interrupted the conversation. "That must be Minnie." Judith jogged to the door, returning moments later with Minnie lagging behind.

Minnie skipped the pleasantries. "Did you bring the goods?"

"I-uh. If you're talking about the lottery tickets, yes." Gloria fumbled around inside her purse and pulled out the small stack of tickets she'd purchased at the Quik Stop. "Thank you for meeting us on such short notice."

Minnie took the tickets and lifted a hand. "First I scratch, then we chat. I need a coin."

Ruth and Gloria exchanged a quick glance and Ruth gave a small shake of the head so Gloria reached inside her change purse, pulled out a dime and handed it to Minnie.

Minnie plopped down in an empty chair and began to scratch the pile of tickets. "There's one here for ten bucks." The trio remained silent; the only sound inside the kitchen was the scraping of the coin against the card. "Got another five bucks."

Minnie tapped the cards on the table and then brushed the shavings from the cards onto Judith's floor.

"I just swept!"

"What?" Minnie rolled her eyes. "It's only a few shavings. Sheesh." She pocketed the tickets and swiveled in her seat. "I know Judith is in a big yank to head out so we'll make this brief. You want the scoop on Vanessa Hines."

"Yes," Gloria nodded. "If you haven't already heard, I found Vanessa's body in her basement, and if that wasn't bad enough, she had a floral arrangement on her dining room table, and the card had my husband's name on it."

Minnie tsk-tsked. "I think someone was trying to frame Paul. Although I didn't work directly with Vanessa, she was...shall we say? Not well liked."

She continued. "According to the rumors I heard, she was on probation for leaving her station during working hours without clocking out, leaving the front desk empty. That's a big no-no."

"Who wrote her up?" Ruth asked.

"Fire Chief, Owen Belkins. Right after he wrote her up, she turned around and filed a sexual harassment suit against him, and a second claim against the co-worker who turned her in for leaving during her shift."

Minnie lowered her voice. "It's a woman."

Gloria's hand flew to her mouth. "You're kidding. She claims the woman was sexually harassing her?"

"Yep." Minnie nodded. "Of course, all of this is secondhand info and not verified. Straight out of Pearl Johnson's mouth. She said Vanessa told her it was all true."

She continued. "My personal opinion is it was all a farce. I don't believe for one second that Vanessa's charge against Lauren was legit. Lauren Dolby is straight as an arrow, and the woman was downright furious when she found out Vanessa had filed a harassment claim. There was also another co-worker Vanessa may have had it in for, but from what I was told, she never filed a claim."

Gloria wondered if Lauren had been angry enough to confront Vanessa and the two became involved in a physical confrontation. "Who was that?"

"Tucker McDonald. Now I gotta say, it's quite possible Tucker put the moves on Vanessa," Minnie said. "I don't think she was the least bit interested because of her obvious obsession with P..." Minnie abruptly stopped. "I'm sorry Gloria, but the woman had the hots for your hubby."

"I...It's okay. I mean, I had no idea, but I can see how a woman could fall for Paul."

"He's a real catch," Ruth chimed in and then shifted the conversation back to Vanessa. "So this gives us two possible suspects with motive. Fire Chief, Owen Belkins and Lauren Dolby."

Gloria opened her mouth to tell the trio about her conversation with Sally Keane and Vanessa's visit to the Quik Stop, how she suspected someone had followed her home but quickly changed her mind. She would wait to share that tidbit of information with the girls.

Judith tapped the top of her watch. "I hate to break up this little meeting, but I'm going to be late for my Pilates class and if I'm late, Eleanor will make me do ten sit-ups and ten pull-ups."

"Gotta lose me about ten more pounds and I'll join the class." Minnie patted her ample hips. "That's why I gave up the goodies. Pearl and I are going to one of those all-inclusive resorts in Mexico next March, and I promised myself I was gonna fit into a two-piece bikini." She shoved her chair back and stood. "Oh. There is one more person I forgot to mention."

"Who?" Gloria asked.

"Vanessa's ex-husband, Miles. They went through a nasty divorce. Vanessa called the cops on him a bunch of times." Minnie lowered her voice. "Now, I'm not supposed to divulge this information, so let's keep this between the four of us, but when I took her calls, those two were screaming at each other, and I could've sworn Miles told Vanessa he was gonna take her out."

Chapter 8

"As in kill her?" Gloria asked.

"I was thinking the same thing, unless I heard it wrong, except Vanessa had a restraining order on him, but then dropped it when he gave her some money," Minnie said. "That's all I know."

Minnie walked to the back door and stepped onto the stoop. "I'll give you one final bit of parting information."

"Which is?" Ruth prompted.

"Miles Hines has a lengthy rap sheet, mostly for assault."

"If I were the police, I would arrest Miles Hines," Judith said. "It's obvious he killed his ex-wife."

"Only problem with that is Miles has been sitting in a jail cell since earlier this week when he was arrested for missing a probation hearing and then getting into a barroom brawl. Course, he coulda had someone on the outside take her out, and he would have the perfect alibi."

The women followed Minnie to her car. "Thanks for the tickets, Gloria."

"You're welcome. Thank you for meeting us on such short notice. You've been very helpful." Gloria turned to Judith. "Thanks for helping us out once again, Judith."

"You're welcome," Judith said. "This is a crummy deal for you. I think you've been set up."

Gloria started to walk to her car and then abruptly halted. She pulled the Michigan Mega Millions ticket she'd purchased from her purse and handed it to Judith. "I picked this up when I bought Minnie's tickets and I want you to have it."

Judith glanced at the ticket. "Thanks Gloria. If I win, I'll give you your dollar back."

"Sounds fair," Gloria chuckled. "I'll be sure to collect if you win." She turned to Ruth. "Meet me at Dot's?"

Ruth gave a thumbs-up. "Yeah. We've got a lot to go on now. I already talked to the others and they're going to meet us there at 6:00."

Gloria could kill two birds with one stone...pick up something for dinner and chat with the girls to go over the list of possible suspects.

She'd just slid behind the wheel and started the car when her phone vibrated. It was Paul. "I thought maybe you ran away from home."

"I thought you ran away this morning," Gloria shot back.

"You can't get rid of me that easy. I figured we both needed some time to calm down. I ran over to the station to see what I could find out. Afterwards, I swung by the farm to check on things."

Paul's farm had sat empty since Gloria and he spent most of their time at Gloria's place.

"It's a good thing I went over there. The washing machine hose started leaking and rotted a few of the floorboards. We can add one more thing to our to-do list."

"Thank goodness you caught it early," Gloria said. They chatted for a few more minutes, and she told him she was on her way to Dot's to pick up food to bring home for dinner. She decided to wait until she got home to mention her visit with Minnie Dexter.

When she reached the restaurant, she exited her car and locked the doors before squaring her shoulders and marching through the front entrance, her head held high.

Gloria Rutherford-Kennedy had nothing to hide. She had not murdered Vanessa Hines in a fit of jealous rage and she would prove it. She met the eyes of several of the diners before making her way to a corner table where Ruth, Lucy, Margaret and Dot were waiting.

She dropped her purse on the table. "Where's Andrea?"

"She's not feeling well," Dot said. "She said to tell you that she's sorry and asked us to give her an update on what is going on in the morning."

"Poor thing. I'll check on her later," Gloria said.

Ray, Dot's husband, swung by with a pot of coffee and Gloria held her hand over the cup. "I think I'll skip the coffee. I'm already wound up tighter than a top, but I will take two of your daily specials, the baked chicken dinner, to take home to Paul."

"Did you two patch things up?" Lucy asked.

"I think so," Gloria said. "At least he's home, and was making jokes when I talked to him."

"Good." Margaret nodded. "This business of him sending Vanessa Hines flowers is nonsense."

Ruth and Gloria took turns sharing what they'd learned from Minnie about the sexual harassment claims, not to mention the fact Vanessa had filed a restraining order against her ex but then dropped it.

"So it's the ex," Dot interrupted. "The police should have an open and shut case."

"Except the ex is in jail and he was at the time of Vanessa's death," Ruth said.

"But it doesn't mean he couldn't have hired someone to take her out, knowing he had the perfect alibi," Gloria said. "I wish I would've jotted down the names of the suspects from the fire department."

"Ah, Gloria is slipping," Lucy teased.

"I remember them," Ruth said. "All of these years of memorizing addresses and names are finally coming in handy."

"I'll get some paper and a pen." Dot shot out of the chair and returned with not only a pen and paper but also Rose.

"I was back in the kitchen prepping for taco Tuesday when Dot told me y'all was out here. What did I miss?"

"The list of suspects." Gloria took the piece of paper and pen from Dot. "First on the list was the woman." She turned to Ruth. "What was her name?"

"Lauren Dolby. She's the one who turned Vanessa in for leaving her post during working hours and then Vanessa turned around and filed a sexual harassment claim against her."

Rose's eyes widened. "For real?"

"According to Minnie, it wasn't true. Vanessa was trying to get even with Lauren," Ruth said. "Next on the list is the fire chief."

"Owen Belkins," Dot said. "He comes in here every once in a while with some of his guys when we have the first responder's appreciation day."

"Wait a minute." Gloria tapped her pen on top of the piece of paper. "Dot. You gave me an awesome idea. We need to find out a little more about the firefighters and anyone else who works for the fire department. Would it be too much to ask you to have another first responder's appreciation day?"

"Of course not." Dot shook her head. "Ray and I have been doing it for a few months now. It was Rose's idea and has been very popular."

"What about Tucker McDonald?" Ruth asked. She turned to Gloria. "Did you catch Minnie's comment about Tucker McDonald possibly hitting on Vanessa?"

"Yeah." Gloria set the pen down and picked up the piece of paper. "We have three solid suspects - Vanessa's ex-husband, the fire chief, and Vanessa's co-worker, Lauren."

The women discussed the suspects at length. The fire department employees had motive since Vanessa named both of them in a sexual harassment claim. They would also know Vanessa's schedule and easily be able to figure out where she lived.

"Too bad we can't get inside Vanessa's house," Lucy said.

"I'm sure the investigators have already gone over her place with a fine tooth comb," Ruth said. "Vanessa was in the post office Saturday, so the incident or head injury occurred sometime between Saturday afternoon and Sunday afternoon when Mally found her body in the basement."

"Sally Keane said Vanessa stopped by the Quik Stop Saturday afternoon and mentioned she thought someone had followed her home from work Friday night," Gloria said. "She also said Vanessa planned to swing by Nails and Knobs to purchase new locks for her doors because she thought someone had been inside her house."

"Our next steps should be to talk to Brian and also set up the first responder's appreciation dinner," Lucy said. "I'll print some flyers for the dinner and drop them off at the fire station tomorrow on my way to the flip house."

"And I'll talk to Brian in the morning," Gloria added.

Ray made his way over to the table and held out a bag. "Here's your food, Gloria."

"Thanks Ray."

"I'm sorry about Vanessa Hines' death." Ray handed her the bag and patted her shoulder. "Dot's been making her rounds today, trying to see if anyone is talking."

Dot shook her head. "Everyone has been talking, but most of it's gossip and guessing. No one seems to have firsthand knowledge of Vanessa Hines."

Gloria handed Ray a $20 bill. "Keep the change. I owe you more than that, especially if you have another appreciation dinner to help me out."

"Is it that time again?" Ray asked his wife.

"It is now," Dot said as she wiggled out of her chair. "We can do a spaghetti and meatball dinner this Thursday at six. It'll give us time to do a little more research."

"I'll get those flyers printed, and Margaret and I can drop them off in the morning," Lucy said.

"Are you getting close to finishing your rehab project?" Rose asked.

"Yes, we're almost done. We're going to plant some bushes and put some fresh bark down before Lucy lists it tomorrow," Margaret said.

"And I'm going to have an open house this Sunday, but I think it's going to go fast," Lucy said confidently. "I priced it aggressively since this is our first flip."

Gloria hadn't seen much of Lucy and Margaret since they started the renovations of the old farmhouse. "Are you going to take on another flip project?"

"Yes," Lucy said. "In fact, Margaret and I have already taken a look at what we hope is our next project. It's a vacant tri-level closer to Green Springs."

"Did you check for bodies?" Gloria joked.

Lucy gave her a dark look. "It's body-free."

"For now," Rose quipped. "Let me know if you want me to run over there with one of my special potions to ward off the evil spirits."

"We'll keep it in mind." Margaret reached for her purse. "I better head home. Tomorrow is going to be a long day."

Gloria thanked her friends for offering to help. After she climbed inside her car, she sent Andrea a quick text to ask how she was feeling and when she got the reply, "queasy and sicker than a dog" her concern heightened.

She left her bag of food on the seat and ran back inside the restaurant where Dot and Rose were cleaning up their table.

Gloria caught Dot's eye. "You're back. Did you forget something?"

"I texted Andrea. She said she's sicker than a dog."

Rose wiped her hands on her apron. "Poor thing. We have some leftover chicken noodle soup from lunch. I'll put some in a container and maybe you can drop it off."

"Chicken soup is a cure-all for everything," Gloria said.

Rose ladled soup into to-go containers and carefully placed the containers in the bottom of a plastic bag before adding napkins and saltine crackers. "Even if Andrea can't stomach the soup, the saltines should help a little."

Gloria thanked them again and carefully carried the food to her car. She set it on the passenger side floor and hopped in before picking up her cell phone to text Andrea. "I have some chicken noodle soup and saltine crackers from Dot's I want to drop off. I won't stay." She didn't wait for a reply and dropped her cell phone in the center console.

As she drove to Andrea and Brian's home, she prayed for her young friend. She hadn't heard of any bugs going around and hoped whatever she had wasn't contagious.

The front porch lights were on when she pulled in the drive. She carefully picked up the bag of food, hurried to the front and rang the doorbell.

Moments later, the door creaked open and Brian stepped onto the porch. "Thanks for stopping by. Andrea is on the sofa in the living room. Do you have time to come in for a moment?"

"I don't want to bother her or you," Gloria said.

"You're not bothering us. Andrea wants to talk to you." Brian motioned Gloria inside the entryway and closed the door behind them. He set the food on a nearby table and led Gloria into the living room.

At first, she didn't see Andrea, who was curled up on the sofa, covered in a thick blanket.

Gloria tiptoed across the room. "Oh dear. I'm sorry you're not feeling well, Andrea. I hope you haven't caught some sort of virus."

Andrea lifted her head. "I'll be okay. I asked Brian to have you come in."

Brian eased onto the edge of the sofa and Gloria perched on an overstuffed chair nearby. Andrea rarely got sick. In fact, she liked to tell the others her mother, a doctor, had killed off so many germs growing up, germs were afraid to come near her.

"What's happening with the investigation?" Andrea whispered.

Gloria briefly recapped all that had happened and ended by telling them Dot planned to hold a first responder's appreciation dinner and invite the suspects.

"Clever," Andrea said.

"And we heard Vanessa suspected someone had been inside her house so she stopped by the hardware store to buy new locks."

"Yes, she did," Brian confirmed.

"We can discuss this later, maybe tomorrow, but first we have to get Andrea on the road to recovery."

Andrea and Brian exchanged a glance. "It might be a while," Andrea said.

"Several more months to be exact," Brian said.

"We're going to have a baby."

Chapter 9

"A baby?" Gloria gasped. "We're going to have a baby? I mean, not me. Oh my gosh!" She sprang from the chair, gently hugged Andrea and then hugged Brian. "When?"

"May," Brian said, grinning from ear-to-ear. "We wanted to wait until we got through the first few months and Andrea thought she would be feeling better by now, but she still has her days."

"Alice is over the moon and hovering like a mother hen. She barely lets me out of her sight."

"Well, you can add a few more mother hens." Gloria clapped her hands. "Wait until the girls hear this. Of course, I'll let you be the one to share the news. Maybe I should bake a baby cake and you can surprise them. I hope you tell them soon. I'm not sure how long I can keep such a wonderful secret."

"Can I tell Paul?"

"Of course," Andrea smiled. "Why don't we plan a get-together Sunday afternoon if that works for you?"

"Yes," Gloria gushed. "I could host a luncheon. Maybe we can have those cute little finger sandwiches along with tea and lots of sweet treats."

"As long as you don't have tuna fish. It makes me gag...the smell, the texture."

"No tuna," Gloria promised. She rambled on for several more moments. "I almost forgot I have food in the car and Paul is home waiting for me." She hugged Andrea again and then Brian walked Gloria to the door.

"If you want to swing by tomorrow, we can chat about Vanessa Hines. Maybe I can recall something she said that will be helpful." Brian followed Gloria onto the porch. "I'm worried about Andrea."

Gloria patted his arm. "If you're concerned, why don't you make an appointment to see the doctor? Perhaps he or she will have tips to help Andrea deal with her morning sickness. Some women only get it for a short time; others get it for longer periods of time, while others don't get it at all."

"I think I will ask her to see the doctor. We're over the moon about the baby, although we'd talked about starting a family, we planned to wait for another year or so."

"God had other plans," Gloria said. "His timing is perfect." She hugged the father-to-be tightly and floated to the car. Despite the past couple of days, nothing was going to get Gloria down.

She drove back to the edge of town and coasted to the stop sign. Gloria looked both ways when the sound of sirens filled the air, followed by bright flashes of light. Moments later, an ambulance roared past and headed out of town.

Gloria followed the ambulance at a safe distance, all the while praying for whoever was inside the ambulance.

The porch light was on when Gloria pulled into the drive. She steered her car into the garage and Paul met her near the side door. "I was getting ready to send out a search party."

"I'm sorry." Gloria handed her husband the bag of food. "I was heading home when I found out Andrea wasn't feeling well, so I stopped by her place to drop off some soup."

"Hopefully there's not a bug going around. It is flu season."

"I don't think we have to worry about getting what Andrea has. She has morning sickness."

"She's pregnant?"

"Yep," Gloria beamed. "But we have to keep it a secret. I'm hoping to have a girl's get-together Sunday afternoon so she can tell the others."

As they walked to the house, Gloria shared the details that she knew. The couple carefully avoided mentioning the earlier incident as they transferred the food from the to-go containers onto dinner plates.

After the table was set and Paul eased into the chair next to his wife, he grasped her hand. "I love you."

"I love you, too." Gloria's throat caught. "Let's not fight again."

"Agreed." Paul squeezed her hand and released his grip as they both bowed their heads. "Dear Lord, thank you for this food. We pray you bless it to our bodies. I pray Vanessa Hines' killer, if there is one, is quickly apprehended. Thank you for the wonderful news of Brian and Andrea's baby. We pray you ease Andrea's morning sickness, and that you keep both her and the baby healthy."

"Thank you for the gift of Your Son, our Savior, Jesus Christ," Gloria finished. She lifted her head and reached for a roll. "The baby is due in May. It will be a long winter waiting for that precious child to make an appearance."

"Are we still planning on visiting Ben, Kelly and the grandkids in Texas this winter?"

"Yes. Now that I've told them, Ariel and Oliver keep asking when Grams and Paul are coming. They would be heartbroken if we didn't make the trip."

"I say we spend at least a week in Texas. We can visit the San Antonio River Walk. I've always wanted to see the Alamo."

The couple discussed several side trips they wanted to take and then the subject drifted to Vanessa Hines' death. Gloria was the one to broach the subject. "Were you able to find anything out about Vanessa's death?"

"Yes. She recently filed harassment claims against the fire chief and a co-worker." Paul peeled a piece of meat from his drumstick and chewed thoughtfully. "It seems the woman had her share of enemies."

"And an ex-husband she filed a restraining order against," Gloria added.

"You've been busy today, too," Paul said. "What did you find out?"

"The same thing you did," Gloria said. "It helps to have connections."

"Pearl Johnson?"

"Nope." Gloria shook her head. "Minnie Dexter. Judith arranged a meeting."

"Maybe you should let Judith join the Garden Girls team," Paul teased.

Gloria frowned. "I wouldn't go that far."

After they finished their food, they loaded the dishwasher and Paul pulled his wife into his arms. "I think we need some of Alice's special salsa."

Gloria chuckled. "Are you hinting that we need to make an early evening of it?"

"Yes, but first I have to make sure I shut everything off in my workshop." Paul reluctantly released his grip. "I'll be right back."

Mally followed him outdoors and while they were gone, Gloria filled her pets' food and water dishes.

She removed her cell phone from her purse and carried it to the counter to plug it into the charger when noticed she'd missed several phone calls. One was from Ruth, a second from Dot and a third from Lucy.

"Uh-oh." Her heart sank as she remembered the ambulance that had passed her on her way home. She tried Dot's cell phone first and it went to voice mail. She tried Ruth's cell phone next, but she didn't answer either.

The third try was the charm and a breathless Lucy answered. "Hi Gloria. Where are you?"

"Home. Why?"

"Judith Arnett was almost run over near the front of her driveway. I guess it happened right after you left her. Carl found her lying on the ground."

***

"Judith was hit by a car?" Gloria began to feel lightheaded. She gripped the edge of the counter to steady herself. "Is she going to be okay?"

"I hope so. Ruth was on her way home after leaving the restaurant when the ambulance tore past her, so she followed it to Judith's house. She has more of the details, but from what I heard, they loaded Judith into the back of the ambulance and headed to the hospital. Carl followed behind in his car."

"Hit by a car?" Gloria whispered. "Judith and Vanessa live less than a block apart. You don't think someone is following women around town, waiting until they're alone and then trying to take them out, do you?"

"I can't imagine," Lucy said. "Thank goodness Carl got home when he did."

"Do they know who the driver was?"

"I don't know," Lucy said.

"How awful. You're not even safe in your own driveway," Gloria said, and a horrible thought ran through her mind. *What if someone had intentionally hit Judith?*

"...so she's on her way to the hospital."

Gloria mentally shook her head. "I'm sorry Lucy. I missed part of what you said."

"Ruth is on her way to the hospital, and she said she would give me a call when she had an update on Judith's condition."

Paul stepped into the kitchen and stood quietly listening to the conversation.

"Please let me know as soon as you hear from Ruth and I'll do the same." Gloria thanked Lucy for the update, ended the call and placed the phone on the counter. "Right after Ruth and I left Judith's house this evening, she was out near the end of her driveway and someone struck her. It sounds like a hit and run."

"Is she going to be okay?"

Gloria repeated what Lucy had told her. "Ruth was heading to the hospital and will let us know when she has an update on Judith's condition." She pulled out a kitchen chair and sank into the seat. "I feel terrible. What are the chances of Judith being mowed down right after Ruth and I left her house?"

Had the driver been spying on them, waiting until the women left and Judith was alone? What if Carl hadn't arrived home when he did?

Gloria closed her eyes and prayed for Judith, that she would be all right. "I've never heard of a hit and run in Belhaven."

"You mentioned Minnie Dexter was there, as well."

"Yes. We didn't stay long, less than half an hour because Judith was headed to Eleanor's for an evening Pilates class."

"You need to be careful wandering around after dark," Paul said. "All of the residents in town need to be on alert."

Gloria's phone chirped again. This time it was Dot, repeating what Lucy had said. "The locals are freaking out. First, Vanessa and a day later, Judith. Everyone is wondering who will be next."

"We all need to be careful," Gloria said. "Judith was on the way to her car when Minnie, Ruth and I left her. What are the chances of her being struck by a vehicle, in a residential area, near the end of her driveway?"

Gloria's phone beeped. She pulled it away from her face and studied the screen. "Ruth is on the other line."

She promised Dot she would call her back before disconnecting the line.

"Hi Ruth. Any news on Judith?"

"Yes and that's why I'm calling you first," Ruth said.

Chapter 10

"First of all, Judith is going to be all right. The driver's passenger side mirror clipped Judith at the top of her shoulder. She fell back, onto her driveway and she hurt her back so the doctors are keeping her overnight for observation to make sure nothing else is going on," Ruth reported.

"What happened?"

"From what Carl told me, Judith said right after we left, she went to the garage to wheel her trashcan to the curb for garbage pick-up tomorrow morning. She said it was dark and she could hear an engine revving at the corner."

Ruth went on to say Judith had just placed the trashcan near the street and turned to go when she saw bright headlights. "Next thing she knew, the vehicle was coming straight towards her. She tried to shield her face and jump out of the way, but the passenger side mirror struck her shoulder and she fell."

"The vehicle never even slowed. Police were still there investigating when I left to follow the ambulance to the hospital. I'm not sure what they found," Ruth said.

"The important thing is Judith is going to recover," Gloria said. "What if it wasn't an accident and someone tried to take Judith out?"

"I was thinking the same thing. The fact that Vanessa and Judith live less than a block from one another is suspect. Maybe some riff raff has moved into Belhaven Corners."

"I hope not. The Lord was surely protecting Judith. Be careful driving home, Ruth," Gloria said. "In fact, why don't you call me when you're home and inside with the doors locked?"

"I'll be fine."

Gloria insisted and Ruth finally relented, promising her friend she would call as soon as she arrived home. "I'm leaving the hospital now. If you could give Lucy a buzz to let her know, I'll call Dot and Margaret."

Gloria promised her she would and then told her friend good-bye.

After calling Lucy and telling her what she knew, Gloria reminded her friend to be on alert both at home and on the roads.

"I'll be careful," Lucy reassured her before saying good-bye.

Gloria placed her cell phone on the counter and turned to her husband. "Thank God Carl came home when he did. Judith was lying in their driveway. What if Carl hadn't seen her and accidentally ran over his own wife?"

The couple wandered into the living room and settled into their recliners. Gloria reached for the remote and turned on the television.

Now that fall was in full swing, she liked to stay up on the weather, so she turned it to the

Weather Channel before switching over to the 24-hour local news.

The news anchor reported on local politics, followed by the weather forecast and then cut to a breaking news story. They showed a live shot of Judith's driveway and several police cars that were parked out front. The reporter called Judith's incident a hit and run, and stated the police were searching the area for a dark-colored pick-up truck with a loud engine.

After the news clip ended, Paul returned his recliner to an upright position and lifted both hands over his head. "It's been a long day. I'm beat so I think I'll get ready for bed."

With all that had happened since she'd arrived home, Gloria had completely forgotten about their "early evening." She set the remote in her lap. "Does that mean you want to take a raincheck on our early evening?"

"Yes." Paul's hands dropped to his side. "Tell you what, why don't we have a nice evening at

Garfield's over on Lake Harmony tomorrow night? We can get away from all of this mess and enjoy a romantic date night."

"That sounds wonderful."

Paul pulled his wife out of the recliner and into his arms. "And there will be no postponing our early evening again."

"I wouldn't dream of it." Gloria snuggled into Paul's arms and placed her cheek on his chest. "I'm ready for this day to end."

Although it was still early, Gloria was exhausted. The disagreement with Paul, questioning Minnie, hearing the wonderful news about Andrea and Brian's baby, not to mention the horrifying news of Judith's hit and run incident, had taken their toll.

Gloria made sure the porch light was off before she let Mally out. She stood near the top step while her pooch patrolled the yard.

Mally attempted to sneak in a second perimeter patrol and Gloria called her to the porch. "C'mon Mally. I'm bushed."

When they were both safely inside, Gloria closed and locked the door behind them.

Puddles greeted her at the door and began circling her legs. She picked him up and held him close. "I haven't seen much of you lately. You spend a lot of time sleeping these days."

Puddles was getting up there in years, and the past few months, Gloria had noticed he was moving slower, as if his joints were stiff. His fur was turning a pale shade of gray and starting to thin.

She wasn't looking forward to the day when Puddles was gone. He had been her constant companion for many years, before Mally and then Paul came along. "I'm going to pick up your favorite treats while I'm out tomorrow," she promised as she scratched his ears and then gently set him on the floor. "But for now, it's time to hit the hay."

***

Sometime during the night, Gloria woke and reached over to touch Paul but his side of the bed was empty.

"Paul?" He didn't answer so Gloria flung the covers back, pulled her robe on and slipped out of the bedroom. She found Mally and Paul in the kitchen, peering out the kitchen window.

"What is it?" she whispered.

"I thought I heard a dull *thunk* a couple of minutes ago while I was in bed. Mally began growling, so we decided to take a look around."

"Do you see anything?"

"No, but it's dark out there." Paul gave Gloria a quick glance. "We really need to put another light out near the barn."

The couple had discussed it on and off for several months. She remembered the time she discovered someone hiding out inside her barn. It was around the time Paul and Gloria met. Actually, the second time she'd seen Paul was when she and her grandsons had spotted someone creeping around the barn. She'd called the Montbay County Sheriff's Department and he'd responded.

"I agree."

Mally pressed her snout against the glass pane and let out a low growl.

"Ah. I see the culprits," Paul said.

Gloria peered over his shoulder. "Where?"

"There. It's a doe and buck, walking across the yard to the field out back."

Woof.

Gloria jumped back and clutched her chest. "Mally, you scared me half to death," she scolded. "It's only deer."

"They're on the move this time of the year. I'm going to get a drink of water before heading back to bed." Paul grabbed two glasses from the cupboard and handed one to his wife. "Are you going hunting with Lucy again this year?"

"No." Gloria turned the faucet on and filled her glass. "I don't plan on it and don't you dare mention it to her."

Lucy had convinced Gloria to go deer hunting with her the previous year. She'd smeared stinky deer lure all over Gloria's clothes before they hopped on Lucy's quad and drove deep into the woods where they climbed up into a tree stand and sat in the cold, dark morning for what seemed like an eternity.

Finally, a buck appeared and Lucy got so nervous, she missed her shot and the buck ran off. "She's so preoccupied with the rehab project; I don't think she's spent much time working on her hunting schedule."

"Maybe Margaret will go with her," Paul said.

"Margaret?" Gloria laughed. "I would pay money to see that."

The couple wandered back to the bedroom and Mally settled into her doggie bed near the dresser. Despite feeling wide awake, Gloria easily drifted off to sleep.

When she woke, she studied the ceiling for several long moments. Her first thought was of Judith and she prayed for a speedy recovery.

Gloria's back began to ache so she shifted onto her side.

Paul opened one eye. "I guess we better get up and at 'em. Daylight is burning."

After making the bed, Mally and Gloria headed to the kitchen to start breakfast and a pot of coffee while Paul made his way into the bathroom.

The couple discussed adding a master bath and larger closet since the old farmhouse only had one indoor bathroom and a small closet.

Gloria didn't relish the thought of tearing her house apart, and they finally decided they were comfortable with the house the way it was.

She let Mally out and began scrambling eggs and frying bacon when Paul appeared. "I'll make the toast."

They chatted about fall, the deer and Judith's hit and run incident before settling in at the kitchen table with their food. Gloria reached for the morning paper and glanced at the headlines. "What's on the agenda today?"

"I'm going to run down to Nails and Knobs to pick up some trim boards to replace the warped boards out at the farm. I don't want to leave it too long, plus I want to make sure it's not leaking again," Paul said. "After that, I thought I would run by to pick up Ryan and Tyler."

Gloria frowned. She'd been so wrapped up in investigating Vanessa's death, she forgot that her grandsons were coming over to help rake the fall leaves.

"It completely slipped my mind." Gloria shook her head. "My goodness. I'm going to have to start keeping a day planner."

Paul patted her hand. "We've had a lot going on. I thought I could run by and get them and then later, when we're ready to head out for dinner, we can drop them off on our way."

Gloria's eyes widened.

"Let me guess. You forgot all about our dinner plans," Paul said.

"Maybe I have the onset of Alzheimer's," Gloria murmured. "I can't believe I forgot both of those things."

"I'll have to start following you around, making sure you're all right," Paul teased.

"Do you really want to do that?"

"No. It was a joke. And, keeping tabs on you would only add to my gray hairs."

"It's not that bad," Gloria argued. "How much trouble do I get into?"

Paul raised an eyebrow.

"Okay. Don't answer that."

Paul shooed his wife out of the kitchen to get ready after she admitted she was chomping at the bit to run down to Dot's Restaurant to get an update on Judith's condition.

They both left the house at the same time with Paul heading to the hardware store. Gloria followed him into town and parked in the post office parking lot before heading inside. For the second day in a row, the lobby was packed.

Gloria squeezed past several locals in an attempt to reach the front counter when she spotted Ruth, who was chatting with Sally Keane.

She started to back away, but Sally caught her eye. "Hello Gloria. Ruth and I were discussing poor Judith's hit and run. I was thinking to myself that maybe it's time to move out of Belhaven. This place isn't safe for a single woman."

"We should be so lucky," Gloria muttered under her breath.

"Perhaps you and Officer Joe should tie the knot," Ruth said.

Sally shifted to the side to make room for Gloria. "We've talked about it on and off, but you know, I would worry about his safety constantly. I'm sure you understand."

"Thankfully, Paul retired right after we wed, although he still does some side security jobs." She remembered the time, not long ago, when he was working security at a local jewelry store, and a couple of teenagers tried to rob it.

Gloria had been horrified while Paul brushed it off. Since the incident, Gloria hoped he would stop working the part-time jobs. His pension, plus both of their retirement accounts and social security had left them in a position to live out the rest of their lives comfortably.

She suspected Paul's real reason for taking the jobs was that it gave him a sense of purpose and something to do. "Do you have an update on Judith's condition?"

Ruth nodded. "Yes. Carl called first thing to let me know the doctors were going to release Judith this morning. Her hand and shoulder are sore and she's having a little back pain but I guess she's anxious to get back home. She's also madder than a wet hornet. I guess she was wearing her favorite bracelet when she was struck. She lifted her arm to cover her face, the vehicle's passenger side mirror caught the edge of the bracelet and it broke."

She continued. "Lucy and Margaret were already in here bright and early. Lucy made some flyers for the first responder's appreciation spaghetti dinner at Dot's, and she and Margaret were going to drop them off. After that, they were heading to the reno to finish a couple small projects and then put a sign in the yard."

Gloria rubbed her brow. "The dinner completely slipped my mind. Thursday. Right?"

"Thursday," Ruth confirmed. "How is Andrea feeling?"

"She's...going to be okay," Gloria avoided Ruth's gaze. The woman had an uncanny ability to read her friends' minds.

"You're sure?" Ruth pressed.

"I'm sure." Gloria glanced at her watch. "My, my apple pie. Look at the time. I better let you get back to work." She dropped her bundle of envelopes in the outgoing mail slot and hurried out of the post office.

She crossed the street and stepped inside Dot's Restaurant where she caught a glimpse of Dot darting back and forth near the server station.

Gloria made her way to the coffee machines and helped herself to a cup.

"I wondered when you were going to show up," Dot said. "Glen Shenk just left. He drove by Carl and Judith's place. It looks like she's home already."

Rose joined the women. "Dot, bless her heart, is gonna take some food over there around lunch time."

"Dot has a heart of gold. By the way, the chicken dinners you sent home last night were delicious."

"You liked the chicken?" Dot beamed. "I'm experimenting with a new recipe."

"It's a keeper," Gloria said. "I was going to run by Nails and Knobs to chat with Brian. Andrea was feeling a little under the weather last night, but I think she's going to be fine."

"Good," Dot said.

"She's a little on the skinny side," Rose said. "We need to fatten her up. One of these days, those kids are going to want to start a family and they're gonna wear her down to nothin'."

Gloria, who had taken a sip of her coffee, began to choke.

"Are you okay?" Rose slapped her on the back.

"It went down the wrong way." Gloria coughed and clutched her chest. "I better let you two get back to work. I'll stop by later to see if Dot has anything new to report on Judith."

She thanked her friends for the coffee and hurried out of the restaurant. Keeping the baby secret was going to be harder than Gloria thought.

Chapter 11

"This is our last stop," Lucy announced as she pulled into the Montbay County Fire Department parking lot and shifted her jeep into park. "Remember the plan."

"I don't know how well this is going to work," Margaret said. "First of all, we don't know if the people Vanessa accused of sexual harassment are even working today. Second, even if they are working and we strike up a casual conversation with them, they're not going to talk to two complete strangers about a dead co-worker. I'm sure the investigators have already been here and questioned them."

"True, but I've got a plan." Lucy handed the first responder's appreciation dinner flyer to Margaret. She reached into her purse and pulled out another sheet of paper. "As Gloria likes to say, I'm going to kill two birds with one stone...post the flyer for the dinner *and* ask if we can post the flyer for our newly-renovated property."

"I can appreciate your resourcefulness, but how will this help with the investigation?"

"Watch and learn." Lucy hopped out of the Jeep and slammed the door shut.

She led the way inside the fire station and approached the front desk. "Hello. I'm Lucy Carlson. My friend, Margaret and I are here on behalf of Dot's Restaurant in Belhaven. We're inviting all of the employees of this fire station to a first responder's spaghetti appreciation dinner at her restaurant this Thursday evening, starting at six."

The woman took the flyer from Lucy and studied the front. "Oh, this is the same sweet lady who hosted an appreciation dinner a couple months back. Some of our firefighters were bummed out because they missed it." She popped out of her chair and hurried to the bulletin board.

"I'll stop back in a couple of days to pick up the paper since there's a sign-up sheet on the bottom. The restaurant will only hold so many people, and we're also inviting the Montbay County Sheriffs, plus the emergency medical responders." Lucy glanced at the placard on the desk, *Lauren Dolby*. Bingo.

"Oh, this thing will fill up in the next day so that won't be a problem." The woman tacked the flyer to the board and made her way back to the desk. "Last time, she had chicken and dumplings. It was delicious. I asked Mrs. Jenkins for the recipe, but she told me it was a family secret."

"That's Dot," Margaret chuckled.

"Are you going to be able to make it...Lauren?" Lucy asked.

"Yes. I work the day shift and my shift ends at five, so I'll be there. Last time, me and some of my co-workers made a night of it, stopping by a small bar a couple doors down from the restaurant before dinner for happy hour."

"At Kip's Bar and Grill?" Lucy asked.

"Yeah. It was a fun evening out, and we'll probably do it again."

Lucy smiled. *Loose lips sink ships.* "It sounds like a great idea. While I'm here, I thought I would drop off a flyer for a property I'm listing tomorrow. I'm a real estate agent and co-owner of *Hip Chick Flips*. We recently renovated a farmhouse near Belhaven and are putting it on the market." She held up the flyer. "Do you mind if I put this on the bulletin board, as well?"

"Not at all." Lauren took the flyer from Lucy and returned to the bulletin board where she tacked the flyer next to the appreciation dinner flyer. She shifted to the side, a somber expression crossing her face. "One of my co-workers, Vanessa Hines, recently moved to

Belhaven. She was murdered a couple of days ago."

"We heard," Margaret said quietly. "We were shocked to hear of her death."

"I saw the news clip on the television," Lucy said. "Such a tragic incident. You said you knew Ms. Hines?"

"Yes. We were co-workers," Lauren said.

Lucy took a step closer. "I'm sure the authorities are working diligently to solve the mystery surrounding Ms. Hines' death."

"They'll be digging around for a while." Lauren started to say something, but then she stopped.

Lucy clasped her hands in front of her. "Do you think Ms. Hines was specifically targeted?"

"It's possible. Although she wasn't well-liked around here, none of her co-workers were involved in her murder," Lauren said. "In fact, I told the authorities that before Vanessa and I had a falling out and were no longer on speaking terms, she confided in me her ex-husband was sending her texts, threatening to have her taken out and boasting that the police would never be able to pin it on him."

Lauren continued. "They went through a bitter divorce and at one time she had a restraining order against him but dropped it. He gave her some cash to let it go."

"Then I'm sure Vanessa's ex is the first suspect the investigators spoke with."

"Yeah, but it'll be hard to pin it on him," Lauren said. "He was in jail at the time of her death and he's still there. My theory is, while Miles was in jail, he hired an ex-con to do the deed, knowing he had a surefire alibi."

"You didn't like Vanessa?" Margaret asked.

"No. She filed some bogus charges against me and my boss after I turned her in for leaving her post during on-duty hours." Lauren twirled her finger near her temple. "Then she became fixated on some old dude, a retired cop who lives in the Belhaven area."

She paused when she realized the man she was talking about, Paul, was the same age as the women she was sharing the story with. "I'm sorry. I didn't mean old, but you know, decades older than Vanessa."

Lucy lifted a hand. "No offense taken."

"I take it you like your boss, the fire chief," Margaret chimed in.

"Fire Chief Belkins is straight as an arrow. He would never say anything or do anything inappropriate to the women who worked for him," Lauren said. "She also threatened to press charges against Tucker. He told me it was because he wouldn't give her the time of day."

"Oh?" Margaret lifted a brow. "She was after an 'old dude' *and* someone named Tucker?"

"Yes. Tucker and I have been dating for a few months now. Vanessa was after him. Finally, he had to point blank tell her he wasn't interested." Lauren confided.

"It was kind of a mess when I reported Vanessa for leaving work while on duty and Chief Belkins put her on probation." Lauren sighed heavily. "I didn't have it in for her, although she thought I did."

The office phone rang.

"We better let you go." Lucy and Margaret thanked Lauren, telling her they would stop back in a couple of days to collect the dinner sign-up sheet before they exited the building.

Lucy waited until they were inside the jeep. "That was an interesting conversation. What do you make of it?"

"On the surface, it appears Vanessa may have been a little unbalanced. She was upset Lauren turned her in, upset when this other co-worker spurned her advances and mad that Chief Belkins put her on probation."

"Then there's the ex who may have hired someone to do her in while he was behind bars," Lucy said. "I would rule out the fire chief."

Lucy steered the jeep onto the main road. "What if, follow me here, Tucker hadn't spurned Vanessa's advances? What if Lauren found out he was two-timing her?"

"A crime of passion," Margaret said. "What if Lauren went to Vanessa's place, there was some sort of physical altercation and Vanessa hit her head? Lauren stormed out of her house, not knowing Vanessa had suffered a serious head injury and then died either that day or the next morning."

"I'm not sure if it's a stretch or not, but I'm not ruling out Lauren or Tucker," Lucy said. "What if Vanessa was after Chief Belkins, too?"

"Gotta love a man in uniform," Margaret said. "I say we don't rule out anyone, including the fire chief. Always suspect the least suspect."

"Well, at least we've got an inside scoop to share with the others," Lucy said. "Now it's time to get back to work."

Chapter 12

Gloria strolled to the other end of Main Street where Brian's hardware store, *Nails and Knobs*, was located. Brian was in the back, waiting on a couple of customers, so she made her rounds, checking out the new inventory.

Brian had managed to retain the charm of the small town store. He'd recently added a whole section of what Gloria called "nostalgia" items. It reminded her of Woolworth's, the old five and dime stores.

There were bolts of bright fabric, an assortment of table lamps and even bins of hard candy. Gloria grabbed an empty paper bag and plastic scoop, filled the bag with root beer barrels, red licorice bites and even picked up some pixie sticks for Ryan and Tyler.

When she finished, she slid the scoop inside the holder, folded the top of the bag and made her way to the counter.

"You missed Paul. He was in here earlier." Brian pointed at the bag of goodies. "You've given up on the Mackinac Island fudge?"

"No way." Gloria placed the bag of candy on the counter. "I decided to take a quick trip down memory lane, plus Ryan and Tyler are coming over to help rake leaves so I thought I would buy some candy for them." She hopped up on the barstool and set her purse next to her. "How's Andrea feeling this morning?"

"Better," Brian said. "She ate a piece of dry toast before I left for work and managed to keep it down."

"Poor thing," Gloria said. "Did you hear about Judith Arnett?"

Brian nodded his head. "Yeah, I stopped by the post office to drop off some packages and Ruth filled me in. Do you think it's somehow connected to Vanessa Hines' death or has something to do with the fact you were at her place right before she was almost mowed down?"

"I don't know what to think," Gloria said. "It's frightening, though. Two incidents in two days. Sally Keane said she's thinking about moving."

"She's been threatening me for months now." Brian shook his head. "Sally has been hinting around that she wants another raise, but it's not in the budget right now. I hope she doesn't quit."

"I hope not for your sake. I'm also here to find out about Vanessa's visit when she bought new locks for her doors," Gloria said. "Did she tell you she wanted to change the locks because she thought someone had been inside her home?"

Brian nodded. "It's not unusual for a new homeowner to change locks. If you think about it, the house sat vacant for some time. She mentioned a lockbox on the front, which means someone, a real estate agent or others, had access to the key."

"This also means they could have easily made a copy and no one would have known," Gloria said.

"I'm not sure if the home was a short sale, foreclosure or regular sale, but if the owner was forced out, you never know what they'll do to get revenge against the bank or the new owner who took their home from them."

"I'm pretty sure it wasn't, but I hadn't considered that angle." Gloria drummed her fingers on the countertop. "Vanessa worked closely with the sheriff's department and someone probably told her she should change the locks. I know I would."

"Me too," Brian said. "The last straw was when she went out to the shed to grab a broom and noticed the door was ajar and she was certain that she'd closed it."

"I wonder if that's the reason she had her cell phone with her when Mally found her," Gloria mused. "She thought someone was on her property. It would make me nervous, not only being in a new home and new town you aren't familiar with, but also worried that someone was lurking nearby."

Brian leaned his elbows on the counter. "She bought new locks for the front and back doors, and picked up several window locks for the first floor windows."

"Rumor has it that she had plenty of enemies," Gloria said. "She filed a sexual harassment suit against one of her co-workers and her boss and filed a restraining order against her ex."

"The ex should be the prime suspect," Brian said.

"He has an ironclad alibi. He's been in jail for several days now." Gloria reached for her purse. "I'm sure the investigators will stop by here to ask questions about Vanessa's purchases."

"They already have. Detective Green was in here first thing this morning."

"Ah, I must be losing my touch." Gloria eased off the stool. "I better head home. Ryan and Tyler will be there soon. How much do I owe you for the candy?"

"The candy is on me," Brian said. "You're still sitting on our big news?"

"Barely." Gloria rolled her eyes. "I'm determined to keep my mouth shut until Sunday, but I'm so excited. The only person I told was Paul."

"We're excited, too. I just wish Andrea was feeling better."

"It will all be worth it in the end. When you hold that baby in your arms for the first time, the memory of all of the bad days will fade away." Gloria thanked Brian for the candy again and exited the store.

Instead of heading straight home, she decided to circle past Vanessa's home.

Vanessa's Buick was still parked in the drive. The front curtains were drawn and the rocking chair on the front porch was gone. She said a small prayer for Vanessa's family and then slowly turned down a side street, driving by Judith and Carl's place. Gloria made a mental note to send flowers and a card.

When she reached the corner, she turned left and drove down Main Street before heading home.

Paul and the boys were in the yard raking. A large pile of leaves circled the towering oak tree.

Ryan was the first to spot Gloria. He dropped his rake and ran across the lawn, almost knocking her over as he hugged her tight.

"My goodness. I think you grew another foot since I saw you last week."

"I've been eating a lot of granola bars and I think they're making me taller."

Gloria placed her arm around Ryan's shoulders and they wandered over to Tyler.

Tyler's interest in the farm was waning. He would much rather hang out with his friends and had recently joined his school's football team.

Ryan, on the other hand, loved the farm. The last time he'd visited, he told Gloria he thought she should get some farm animals. His reasoning was, if you lived on a farm, you needed to have animals. When she asked him what kind, he told her she could start with some cows, pigs and chickens and then he offered to help her build the pens.

Not wanting to dampen his enthusiasm, she told him she'd think about it, but there was no way Gloria could handle taking care of livestock. If Ryan still loved the farm when he was an adult, she would be more than happy to turn over the reins.

Tyler gave his beloved Grams a quick hug and continued raking.

Paul made his way over and kissed his wife's cheek. "We swung by the fast food joint and picked up some burgers and fries."

"I'm starving," Ryan grumbled.

"It's all of those growth spurts," Gloria teased. "We better get inside and eat. I don't want you passing out from hunger."

The trio propped their rakes against the tree and followed Gloria into the kitchen. The smell of greasy French fries filled the air and her stomach grumbled.

The trio washed up while Gloria filled glasses with ice and set a bottle of Coke on the table. Paul was the first to return and he hugged his wife.

"Wow. I love all the attention."

"It's date day," Paul joked. "Which means you get lots of extra attention."

Gloria bounced up on her tiptoes and kissed Paul on the lips.

"Yuck," Ryan marched into the kitchen.

"Too much PDA," Tyler chimed in.

Gloria handed her eldest grandson a stack of paper towels. "It's KDA, not PDA. Kitchen Display of Affection. Better watch out or I'll start smooching on you."

Tyler wrinkled his nose and shook his head.

The four of them pulled out chairs and sat. Gloria folded her hands and bowed her head while Paul prayed over the food, offering a special prayer for Vanessa's family as well as Judith's speedy recovery.

Ryan and Tyler each polished off two cheeseburgers and a large order of fries before Gloria finished her single patty burger and small fry. The boys excused themselves and headed back out, leaving Paul and Gloria alone in the kitchen.

"I had a moment to talk to Jill while the boys were grabbing their stuff." Paul reached for a

French fry. "She said she was on the fence about letting Tyler come over today but figured a little manual labor might do him some good."

"Oh?" Gloria raised a brow. "Is Tyler grounded?"

"Yes. According to Jill, he got into an argument with his math teacher, called him a few choice names and was suspended from school."

"Oh dear. I think he sometimes has trouble controlling his emotions. Did I ever tell you about the time he pulled the fire alarm at the school?"

"No, but I'm not surprised," Paul said. "I figured raking the leaves wouldn't take us too long, so I promised the boys we could head over to Lake Terrace to do a little fishing."

"That's so thoughtful of you." Gloria smiled at her husband. "Greg tries to do things with the boys, but he's busy at work and has been working a lot of overtime."

Paul picked up a French fry and dipped it in his catsup. "Jeff was a rebellious one, a lot like Tyler." He polished off his fries and crumpled the paper. "I better get out there so we can finish raking."

Gloria hugged her husband, grateful for a man who generously spent his free time with her grandchildren. She swallowed the lump in her throat and gave him a watery smile. "Thank you."

"Don't start crying now."

"I won't," Gloria promised. She finished tossing the food wrappers in the trash before emptying the drink glasses and washing them in the sink.

After she finished, she pulled on an old pair of stained blue jeans and a t-shirt before joining them for the raking project. The four of them made quick work of the task and after they finished, Gloria handed each of them twenty-five dollars.

"Thanks Grams." Ryan shoved the money in his front pocket. "Now can we go fishing?"

"Yes, now we can go fishing," Paul said.

"Make sure you have life jackets in the boat."

Paul gave his wife a thumbs-up before pulling his car to the side of the barn.

While Paul hooked up the small fishing boat, Gloria packed some bottled waters in a cooler and carried it to the car. "Have fun." She hugged Ryan. Tyler was already in the car and Gloria walked Paul to the driver's side. "Be careful."

"We will." He gave his wife a peck on the cheek before climbing behind the wheel. She waited in the drive until they pulled onto the road and then headed inside.

Her first task was to order flowers for Judith and the floral shop promised they would deliver them later that same day. Afterward, she wandered aimlessly through the house and then decided she would make a quick trip to check out Margaret and Lucy's renovation project.

She grabbed her purse and made her way down the steps when she heard an engine revving. Gloria caught a glimpse of something pink out of the corner of her eye.

It was Eleanor's Cadillac. The car veered into the driveway, careened around the circular drive and came to an abrupt halt in front of the porch.

Gloria took a quick step back as the car stopped mere inches from the bottom porch step. She grinned as Eleanor hopped out of the car and sprinted around the front. "I've been trying to track you down all morning."

"Cute outfit." Gloria pointed at Eleanor's hot pink sunglasses, matching scarf and pair of skinny jeans.

"Thanks. I got the jeans from my youngest granddaughter. She was packing up some clothes to sell at a local resale shop. When I saw these, I decided to try them on and they fit."

Eleanor shifted to the side. "You don't think they look too tight do you?"

"Absolutely not," Gloria shook her head. "I think you look adorable. Now you'll have to find a boyfriend."

Eleanor blushed. "Well, a couple of the gals in my Pilates class and I are going to head over to the American Legion in Green Springs this Saturday for the dance. Most nights they have country music, but Saturday night they feature an Elvis impersonator." Her eyelids fluttered and she clutched her chest. "I love Elvis."

"It sounds like fun," Gloria said. "Why were you looking for me?"

"Well, I got a little insider info on Vanessa Hines. Last week her cousin, Doris Tipple, well, it's her second cousin, by marriage." Eleanor waved a hand. "It's complicated. Anyhoo, she told me Vanessa was trying to blackmail her boss, the fire chief."

"Did she mention sexual harassment charges?" Gloria asked.

"No." Eleanor shook her head. "Doris didn't mention charges, only that Vanessa hated her boss."

"Among others," Gloria murmured under her breath.

"It's a shame. Doris said Vanessa became a real health nut the last couple of years, almost to the point of obsession. She would've been the perfect Pilates team leader, and I could've ramped up my exercise classes."

Eleanor shook her keys. "I'm on my way to check out Margaret and Lucy's flip property. My daughter and her husband are thinking about moving out of the city, and they want to live closer to me. I remembered you mentioning the place Margaret and Lucy fixed up."

"I was going there myself," Gloria said.

"Great. You can ride with me."

"I can drive myself."

"But I'm parked behind you," Eleanor argued. "Plus, I need more driving practice. I'm getting better, although still a little off when calculating my speed on sharp turns but other than that, I think it's like riding a bike. You never forget how to do it."

Gloria glanced at Annabelle and then at the eager look on Eleanor's face. "I guess I can ride with you." She briefly closed her eyes, certain that she was going to regret her decision.

Chapter 13

"If you're sure," Gloria said. "I don't mind driving."

"I'm positive." Eleanor darted around the front of the car.

Gloria opened the passenger side door and peered inside.

"Don't mind the mess." Eleanor tossed an empty Starbucks cup, a hairbrush, a padded black bra and several packets of Kleenex into the backseat. "I cleaned the car out the other day, but you wouldn't know it."

Gloria rolled a can of Aqua Net hairspray out of the way and gingerly slid onto the passenger seat. She pulled the door shut and began to pray.

"Oh, the side seatbelt doesn't work. I think it's jammed. I need to take the car down to Gus' shop and have him take a look at it." Eleanor grabbed the can of hairspray and tossed it over her shoulder. "The center buckle works fine, if you don't mind sitting next to me."

Gloria had two choices. She could ride with Eleanor sans the seatbelt, but quickly dismissed the idea. She slid to the center and reached for the buckle.

Eleanor started the car and shifted into gear before stomping on the gas pedal.

The house passed by in a blur and Gloria heard a small popping noise coming from the vicinity of her neck as her head snapped back.

When they reached the end of the driveway, Eleanor slammed on the brakes causing Gloria's upper body to fly forward, her forehead grazing the top of the dashboard.

"I think the brakes are bad." Eleanor gripped the steering wheel and leaned forward as she looked in both directions. "I'm going to have Gus check those, too. They're making an awful grinding noise."

Gloria leaned back and gingerly touched her forehead. "They're probably worn out."

"Could be. I haven't had them looked at since I last drove the car several years back. Or they might just need a little adjusting." Eleanor stomped on the gas, and the car lurched onto the main road.

Gloria tightened the strap on the lap belt and began to pray again. Surely, God did not plan for her life to end, sitting shotgun in the front seat of Eleanor's Cadillac. "Yes, you should. The sooner, the better."

She kept her eyes closed for the majority of the trip and almost burst into tears when Eleanor slammed on the brakes and announced, "We're here."

Gloria opened her eyes. Sure enough, they had reached Margaret and Lucy's renovation project and were parked next to Lucy's jeep.

Eleanor peered out her side window. "Looks like I got a tad too close on the driver's side. I don't think I'll be able to open the door. We'll have to get out on your side."

"Sure." Gloria's hand shook as she fumbled with the seatbelt.

Lucy and Margaret, who were planting bushes near the front of the house, wandered over as Gloria slid across the seat and Eleanor followed behind.

Margaret shaded her eyes as Gloria stumbled out of the car. "You two look awfully cozy."

"The passenger-side seatbelt is jammed," Gloria said.

Lucy snorted. "I believe it." She smiled at Eleanor. "Well, look at you, Eleanor. I love the outfit."

"Thanks." Eleanor beamed. "My granddaughter gave it to me." She shifted her gaze. "So this is the place? It looks awesome. I'd like to take some pictures to send to my daughter. They're selling their house in town and want something ready to move into with some land."

"I'll take you on a tour." Lucy linked arms with Eleanor, and they began walking toward the house.

Gloria started to follow behind. Margaret held out her arm and stopped her. "Do you have some kind of death wish, getting in the car with Eleanor?"

"I...didn't want to hurt her feelings," Gloria whispered.

"So how is her driving? I know her stopping and starting skill set is a little rusty."

"I don't know. I had my eyes closed the entire time. I'm surprised she passed her driver's exam."

"She didn't," Margaret said. "Eleanor told me she's driving around with an expired license because she's afraid she won't pass the driving test."

Gloria's eyes grew wide. "Does that mean she doesn't have car insurance either?"

The conversation ended when they reached the porch where Lucy was pointing out some of the features of the home. "Let's head inside."

Gloria had visited the property a few times, but it had been a while, and she was impressed by the transformation that had taken place. "You two did a wonderful job."

"Thanks," Lucy said. "We worked hard on it. Hopefully all of our hard work will pay off."

"I didn't know if I was up to the task," Margaret added, "but it has been therapeutic, a sense of accomplishment, I guess."

"So I take it you're on board to tackle another fixer-upper?" Gloria asked.

"Yes, as soon as we sell this one," Lucy said. They continued their tour into the large country kitchen with an open eating area and a set of sliders. "It was dark in here, so we decided to open it up."

Gloria peered through the slider at the new wooden deck. She smiled as she remembered the time Lucy had blown out the back porch using her homemade explosives.

The women retraced their steps and climbed the stairs to the second floor. The old linoleum flooring was long gone and in its place were dark hardwood floors that ran the length of the hall and continued into the bedrooms.

At the end of the hall was a second bathroom. Gloria stood in the doorway and looked inside.

"We moved some stuff around and found out we had enough room to add double sinks," Margaret said.

Lucy eased past Gloria and tapped the edge of the tub with the tip of her shoe. "Check out the claw foot tub. We found this at an estate sale."

"It's gorgeous." Eleanor lifted her cell phone and snapped a picture of the bathroom. "It's unusual for old farmhouses to have a full bath downstairs and a full bath upstairs. I can't wait to send the pictures to Jodi."

They wandered down the stairs and stepped out onto the front porch. "Even if Eleanor's daughter doesn't want this place, I'm sure you won't have any trouble selling it," Gloria said.

"I don't think so either," Lucy agreed.

"Have you heard how Judith is doing?" Margaret asked.

"No. I drove by her place earlier and saw both her and Carl's vehicles in the drive. I sent flowers."

Lucy wrinkled her nose. "I wish I would've thought of that."

"Don't worry. I put all of our names on them," Gloria said.

"Thanks Gloria. Margaret and I dropped off the flyers for the appreciation dinner at Dot's this Thursday."

"We also did a little intel work while we were at the fire department," Margaret said. "Lucy had a brilliant idea."

"I took a flyer for this property and asked them if I could post it on their bulletin board at the fire department," Lucy said. "As luck would have it, Lauren Dolby was working and we struck up a conversation with her."

"You did?" Gloria asked. "What did she say?"

"It was an enlightening conversation." Lucy went on to tell Gloria and Eleanor about Vanessa's interest in a co-worker, Tucker McDonald, and how he rebuffed her advances, telling her he and Lauren had recently started dating.

"I thought she was in love with Paul," Gloria said.

"Maybe she had the hots for both of them," Margaret said. "Before Vanessa filed charges against Lauren and they were still on speaking terms, Vanessa confided in Lauren that her ex was sending her threatening texts."

"So maybe he hired a hit while he was in jail, knowing he had an ironclad alibi," Lucy said.

"It's a possibility, but it doesn't rule out Lauren," Gloria said.

"Or Tucker," Lucy nodded. "What if Tucker was playing both women and Lauren found out? She got into an argument at Vanessa's place and Vanessa fell or hit her head. Lauren stormed out; not knowing Vanessa's head injury would be fatal."

"That's one theory," Gloria agreed. "What if Lauren and Tucker decided to take Vanessa out because she named Lauren in her sexual harassment complaint and threatened charges against Tucker? The ex would be the perfect scapegoat."

"Maybe we'll get lucky and they'll both show up for the appreciation dinner," Margaret said.

"Lauren told us she would be there. If she's dating Tucker, he'll probably be there too."

"I hope so," Gloria thanked them for the tour before Eleanor and she headed back to the car.

Eleanor climbed in the passenger side first and then crawled to the driver's side. Gloria waited until she was behind the wheel before scooching to the center of the seat and picking up the lap belt.

She spotted Margaret holding her cell phone, taking a picture of Eleanor and her cozied up together.

Gloria wagged her finger at Margaret and Lucy and they both started to laugh before turning around and heading inside.

The drive back to town was similar to the drive to the property, and all done with Gloria's eyes shut.

"Well, lookee over there." Gloria could feel the car slow and opened her eyes.

"Look at what?" They were coasting past Vanessa's place.

"There's some sort of notice hanging on the front doorknob," Eleanor said.

Gloria leaned forward to study the front porch. "I wonder what it is. Could be anything, a utility notice, sorry we missed you."

Eleanor nodded. "The *Meals on Wheels* people left similar notes on my door if they missed me. You want to check it out?" She didn't wait for an answer and swung into Vanessa's drive. "We better hurry before someone sees us."

Gloria slid across the seat, hopped out of the car, darted around the front and sprinted up the steps. She leaned forward and squinted her eyes. It was from the local power company.

She peered inside and pulled out an envelope. The envelope wasn't sealed, so she reached inside and pulled out the folded sheet of paper.

"That's interesting," Gloria whispered before replacing the notice, jogging back to the car and jumping inside. "It was a shut off notice from Consumer's Power. They're shutting off the electric for non-payment."

"Wow. And the power company just stuck it on the door?" Eleanor backed out of the driveway and onto the street.

"It was in an envelope, but it wasn't sealed so I glanced at it," Gloria said. "I wonder if the electric company forwarded the bill from Vanessa's last home and now they're threatening to shut it off where she lives now."

"They'll have a hard time collecting the money," Eleanor said. "I hope you don't mind if I swing by the post office and drop off some mail."

Gloria's eyes flew open. Although it was safety first, she didn't want to ride down Main Street, cozied up next to Eleanor. She reached for the belt buckle, but it was too late. They were already halfway down the main drag, thanks to Eleanor's lead foot.

"There's Bea." Eleanor honked her horn and waved.

Gloria flung herself onto the seat to hide.

Eleanor stopped in the middle of the street and rolled down the window. "Are you going to the dance with us Saturday night?"

Gloria covered her eyes, hoping Bea hadn't spotted her.

"Yes, I think I will." Bea stuck her head inside the driver's side window. "Hi Gloria. I thought that was you."

"Yeah, I...uh dropped my purse." She picked up her purse and slid away from Eleanor.

"We just left Lucy and Margaret's flip house. Have you seen it? The girls did a wonderful job," Eleanor gushed.

Honk. Honk.

Eleanor glanced in her rearview mirror. "I guess I better get out of the street. See you Saturday." She gave Bea a jaunty wave before peeling out and swerving into the post office parking lot. "I'll be right back."

Gloria slouched down in the seat and peered over the dashboard. She could see Eleanor through the large picture window as she waved her hands in the air. Ruth was behind the counter, and she leaned forward as she listened intently to something Eleanor said.

She watched as Eleanor exited the post office and opened the car door. "I told Ruth we went to check out Lucy and Margaret's flip house and when Ruth asked where you were, I told her you were hiding in the car."

"I wasn't technically hiding. More like keeping a low profile," Gloria said.

"I didn't mean to embarrass you."

"You didn't embarrass me, Eleanor. Your driving style took a few minutes to get used to, but I'm definitely not embarrassed." Gloria sat up. "You have to admit that if you spotted two women sitting close together in the front seat of a car you would do a double take."

"True." Eleanor shifted into drive, and for the first time since Gloria got in Eleanor's car, she slowly pulled out onto the street. "I stopped caring what people thought years ago. You should give it a try."

Gloria patted Eleanor's arm. "Ah...Eleanor's words of wisdom." She slid to the center of the seat and reached for the belt buckle. "You know what? You're absolutely right."

Eleanor turned into Gloria's driveway and coasted to a stop.

"Your driving skills are improving," Gloria complimented.

"Thanks," Eleanor beamed. "You're the first person brave enough to ride in the car with me."

"I am?" Gloria reached for her purse. "I'll be happy to ride in the car with you again, my friend, just as soon as you get a valid driver's license." She winked at Eleanor before climbing out of the car. "Thanks for the wild ride."

Chapter 14

Gloria was looking forward to a romantic evening with Paul. It had been some time since they'd gone out on a date, not counting dinners at Dot's place.

After taking a long, leisurely bath, she changed into a new outfit she'd been saving for a special occasion, applied a little light makeup, pulled her hair up in a style Paul loved and then spritzed some of her favorite perfume on both wrists and her neck.

After she finished getting ready, Paul and the boys still hadn't arrived home, so Gloria puttered on the computer, checked her email and then decided to give her daughter, Jill, a quick call to chat about Tyler.

Jill didn't answer so Gloria left a message and headed to the porch with Mally. She eased into the rocker when her cell phone rang. It was Jill.

"Hi dear."

"Is everything okay?" Jill asked. "Is Tyler giving you trouble?"

"Tyler isn't here. After the boys finished raking, Paul took them fishing."

"Good. I mean, I'm glad that he hasn't caused you any grief."

Gloria detected a note of relief in her daughter's voice. "I called to chat about Tylcr. Paul mentioned something about him getting into trouble at school."

"Yes. He's been suspended for two days for yelling at his math teacher," Jill said. "He's frustrated because he's struggling in math."

"Have you thought about hiring a tutor?"

"The tutoring starts next Monday. If one-on-one tutoring doesn't work, we're considering moving him to a private school. We haven't told him yet."

"How do you think he'll react?"

"He'll hate it. These last few months have been difficult. Our loving son has turned into an angry, impatient person and we're beside ourselves."

"I'm sorry." Gloria told her she would be praying for them and watched as Paul's car pulled into the drive. "They're back. We'll drop the boys off in a little while. Paul is taking me to Garfield's for dinner."

"Ooh-la-la," Jill teased. "I heard. I'll see you soon."

Gloria set the phone inside the house and stood in the drive as Paul steered the car to the side of the barn. He unhooked the trailer and pushed the boat next to the barn while Tyler and Ryan showed Gloria their cooler full of fish.

"We caught a batch of bluegill," Ryan said. He reached into the bucket and pulled out a fish. "Paul said he's gonna clean them and filet them and next time we come over, we're gonna have a fish fry."

"Sounds like fun," Gloria said. She turned to Tyler. "How many did you catch?"

"Almost all of them," Ryan answered. "Paul called Tyler the fish whisperer."

Tyler grinned. "I guess they liked my lures better."

Paul lowered the trailer jack, slipped the lock in place and snapped it shut before joining them. "Tyler is a natural fisherman if I ever saw one. He said he'd like to try ice fishing with me this winter."

"Me too," Ryan chimed in.

"You too," Paul ruffled Ryan's hair. "He's the second best fisherman. I only caught a couple."

Ryan chattered excitedly about the lake, the boat, the fish and the different lures as they walked across the yard.

"I guess I better get cleaned up," Paul said.

"Grandpa Paul said you're going on a hot date," Ryan said.

Gloria winked at her husband. "Yes, we are."

The trio sat at the kitchen table chatting about fishing, fall, the upcoming holidays and Christmas. "Mom said you're going to visit Uncle Ben and Aunt Kelly in Houston," Tyler said. "Can we go?"

Jill's boys had never visited their aunt, uncle and cousins in Texas. "Maybe. Let me talk it over with Paul, your parents, and Uncle Ben and Aunt Kelly."

"Talk over what?" Paul wandered into the kitchen.

"Tyler asked if he and Ryan could go to Texas with us to visit Ben, Kelly and the kids."

"Can we?" Ryan bounced in his seat. "I've never been to Texas."

Gloria and Paul's eyes met over Ryan's head. "We'll have to talk to your parents and Uncle Ben and Aunt Kelly, but I'm okay with it."

"Yipee." Ryan sprang from his seat and danced around the kitchen floor.

Even Tyler smiled. "Thanks Paul."

"Thank you," Gloria whispered to Paul as the boys headed outdoors. "Hopefully we won't regret it."

Ryan did most of the talking on the drive to their house while Tyler sat staring out the window, his chin in the palm of his hand. Gloria caught his eye in the rearview mirror, and he gave her a half-hearted smile.

Ryan was the first one out of the car and met his mother in the driveway. "Did you have a good time?"

"We caught a thousand fish," Ryan said. "And Grams said we can go to Texas with her and Paul."

"She did?" Jill lifted a brow. "Are you serious?"

"I'll need to run it by Ben and Kelly and of course, the decision is yours," Gloria said. "We'll have to plan it during the boys' school break, too."

"I'm hungry." Ryan darted into the house, and Tyler slowly followed behind. He turned back. "Thanks for taking us fishing."

"You're welcome. We'll do it again soon," Paul promised.

Jill waited until her eldest son was inside the house and the door closed behind him. "Are you sure you want to take the boys all the way to Texas?"

"Tyler asked and the boys seemed so excited," Gloria said. "Of course, as I said, we'll have to check with Ben and Kelly."

"Maybe they'll forget about it," Jill said.

"And maybe not." Paul nodded toward the door. "I think Tyler enjoyed our fishing trip. He caught more fish than Ryan and I put together."

"I can't remember the last time Greg took the boys fishing," Jill's shoulders sagged. "Or the last time he did anything with them. He's working so many hours down at the shop. They sent out another round of layoff notices and Greg's workload is brutal."

"I'm sorry to hear that," Gloria said. "The boys were on their best behavior. We'll have them over again soon."

She hugged her daughter, and then Paul and Gloria slowly made their way to the car. "It sounds as if Tyler is crying out for his father's attention," Paul said.

"Ryan too," Gloria fretted. "They need money to live on, but we both know those boys will be grown and gone in the blink of an eye."

"Yes, they will."

They rode in silence the short distance to Garfield's, a magnificent bed and breakfast/restaurant located on the shores of Lake Harmony. The restaurant was quiet for a Tuesday evening, and the hostess seated them in an alcove in front of a bay window. Their table featured an unobstructed view of Lake Harmony.

When their teas arrived, Paul lifted his glass. "Here's to the most beautiful woman in the room."

"I'm the only woman in the room," Gloria said.

"That's beside the point."

Gloria decided on a pan-seared whitefish with a side of steamed asparagus and a baked potato while Paul ordered a New York strip, garlic mashed potatoes and green beans.

The server jotted the order on her notepad and after she left, the couple discussed the trip to Texas, the boys' fishing trip, the repairs to the laundry area at Paul's place and then the conversation drifted to Judith's hit and run.

"Maybe the driver didn't see her and panicked when he realized he'd clipped her," Gloria said. She told Paul about her conversation with Brian, how Vanessa believed someone had been inside her home.

Paul sipped his tea and set his glass down. "While you were doing that, I tracked down the name of the flower shop, the one where I supposedly sent flowers from."

"And?"

"It's a small place over in Green Springs. I called and spoke with the owner. She told me she recognized Vanessa's picture from a local news story. Vanessa purchased those flowers herself."

Chapter 15

Gloria frowned. "It doesn't make sense. Does that make sense to you?"

"Not at all. In fact, it sounds a little unstable to me, not that I want to speak ill of the dead."

The server returned with their salads, and they ate in silence as Gloria mulled over what Paul told her. Perhaps Vanessa had been unstable. Who, in their right mind, would move to a town where they knew very few people to be near a married man?

Despite the fact that Vanessa purchased her own flowers, it still didn't mean she hurt herself. She'd obviously been concerned someone was on her property, concerned enough to change all of the door locks and add window locks.

Then there was Judith's incident, less than a block from Vanessa's home. Gloria felt in her bones the two were somehow related.

Could it be the stranger who attacked Vanessa was still lurking in the neighborhood? Gloria hoped during Thursday's spaghetti supper with the first responders, she could find out more about Vanessa Hines. "Dot is holding a first responder's appreciation dinner Thursday evening and I offered to help."

"Let me guess, she invited Montbay County Fire Department staff," Paul said.

"And the Montbay County Sheriffs, too." Gloria finished her salad, placed the fork inside the empty bowl and set it off to the side. "We can kill two birds with one stone. Do a good deed and also perhaps have a chance to chat with the local responders about poor Vanessa's demise."

"Tread carefully," Paul warned. "Detective Jack Green is all over this case."

"So are the Garden Girls."

Their dinners arrived, and Gloria slid a small piece of her fish onto her bread plate and passed it to Paul while he cut a piece of steak off and handed her the fork.

Gloria sampled the meat. "It's delicious, but I'm sure my fish is better." She took a big bite of fish, savoring the rich lemon butter sauce. "I think I'll try to copy this recipe using the bluegills you and the boys caught."

Gloria finished half her fish before leaning back in her chair and patting her stomach. "I'm full."

"Me too."

The server returned to the table. "Would you care for dessert?"

"Heavens no," Gloria said. "But we will take a couple to-go containers."

"Certainly." The server removed the plates of food and returned with two containers.

"Thank you." Gloria inspected her to-go container. "This looks different."

"It is. We just started using them. They're 100% biodegradable and compostable, not to mention microwave safe, unlike the old Styrofoam containers."

"I need to save this and show it to Dot," Gloria said. "She's been talking about trying to increase the amount of items she can either reuse or recycle."

"Are you sure you want to pass on dessert? Perhaps you would like a cup of coffee instead?"

"I've changed my mind," Paul said. "We'll have both."

"We will?"

"There's a white chocolate bread pudding on the menu and it's calling my name."

"It's our most popular dessert," the server said. "If you'd like, I can split an order."

"I suppose," Gloria said.

"Great. One white chocolate bread pudding coming right up." The server turned to go.

"And coffee," Gloria said.

"Two," Paul chimed in.

The dessert arrived warm, and Gloria took the first bite. The creamy white chocolate melted in her mouth. "This is definitely worth the extra thousand calories."

She took another bite and then handed the plate to her husband. After finishing the decadent dessert and drinking their coffee, Paul paid the bill and they wandered out of the restaurant.

"Let's head down to the lake." Gloria tucked her arm in Paul's arm. "I think it would be nice to live on a lake."

"We could sell both the farms and buy a place on Lake Terrace."

"Ryan would never forgive me. As tempting as that sounds, I can't part with my farm and you can't part with yours."

Gloria scanned the horizon, drinking in the peaceful calm of the water. A loud, rattling bugle call echoed across the lake. "It sounds as if we still have a few sandhill cranes who haven't migrated south for the winter."

A cool breeze blew across the open water and Gloria shivered.

Paul placed an arm around her shoulders. "We should head home." When they reached the car, he held the door while Gloria climbed in. She slid to the center and grinned as she remembered riding next to Eleanor.

She waited until Paul was behind the wheel. "Did I tell you that I rode out to Margaret and Lucy's renovation project with Eleanor Whittaker?"

"She renewed her driver's license after all these years?"

"Not yet," Gloria said. "I told her she needed to get a valid driver's license, but I think she's afraid she might not pass the written test, the eye test, the driving portion of the test or all three."

"Do you think she'll pass?" Paul asked.

"If she starts obeying the speed limit, slows down when turning corners and stops slamming on the brakes, there's a chance."

The couple chatted easily during the drive home, and Paul told her his next security detail started in a couple of weeks, when the holiday shopping season kicked into high gear. He would be working at the new outdoor mall in nearby Rockville.

"For how long?" Gloria asked.

"All the way through the holiday season until January 2nd if I want to, but I thought before I committed to the whole season, I would try it first. You can come visit me and shop there."

"It will give me a good excuse to check it out."

When they reached the house, Paul took Mally outdoors while Gloria stored the leftovers in the fridge. She waited until the two of them returned before feeding her pets. "I'm ready to turn in if you are."

"Sounds good to me," Paul said. "Before another crisis comes knocking on our door." He flipped the light off and slid his arm around his wife's waist. "We should turn in early more often."

"You must have read my mind. I was thinking the exact same thing."

***

The next morning, Gloria was up early. Paul and she had a lengthy to-do list, including running over to his farm to clean up the yard. Thankfully, there were a lot less leaves to rake and the washer hadn't sprung another leak.

They wandered around the house and then onto the front porch. "It's such a shame to have the house sit empty. Jeff and Tina have finally settled into the mobile home park and Allie loves her new place. Maybe we should finish sprucing it up and rent it out."

"We could," Gloria said. "It would give us some extra money coming in each month and having the house occupied would save us from having to run over here all the time."

"Do you think Lucy would help us post an ad?"

"I'm sure she would be happy to help and could maybe even help us with the paperwork." The more Gloria thought about it, the more it made sense.

Paul locked the doors while Gloria tossed a bag of trash in the bin.

The idea of renting the property was a bit of a concern. Gloria had heard nightmare stories of people who became landlords and regretted it, but maybe Lucy could help them weed through the applicants to find the perfect tenants.

When they reached Gloria's farm, Paul headed to the workshop to cut some trim boards to replace the ones that had warped from the washer leak.

Gloria decided to call Dot. "Are we still on for the spaghetti dinner Thursday?"

"Yes, and we're going to have a full house" Dot said.

"How do you know?"

"Lucy's sign-up sheets. She picked them up this morning on her way to her flip house and then dropped them off at the restaurant on her way home. "

"Honestly, I forgot all about Lucy's flyers. I was too freaked out from riding in Eleanor's car. By the time we pulled into the drive at Margaret and Lucy's reno project, it completely slipped my mind."

"You rode in Eleanor's car?" Dot laughed.

"It was an adventure. I told Eleanor she needed a valid driver's license before I rode with her again."

"She doesn't have a driver's license?"

"No, and I didn't know that until after the fact," Gloria said. "So what do Lucy's flyers look like?"

"At the top of the flyer is a picture of spaghetti and meatballs with a banner line thanking first responders and inviting them to a complimentary dinner Thursday evening at 6:00. Below the banner is a sign-up sheet."

"You said she dropped them off. So you have a complete list of the people who signed up?" Gloria was itching to get her hands on the list.

"Yes. Lucy, bless her heart, labeled each list. I have one from the Montbay County Fire Department and the sheriff's department. She also put one up at the EMS Station."

"The EMS station, as in emergency medical services personnel?" Gloria asked. "I forgot about them."

"Me too. Eighty-two people signed up. We'll be packing them in like sardines."

"I'm sure a few won't show," Gloria said.

"For a free meal? No, I think we'll have close to 100% turnout."

"I feel bad that you have to cook all of the food for free. At least let me write you a check to cover the cost of the food."

"That's thoughtful of you Gloria, but not necessary. My accountant has figured out a way for me to write off the food, pay the hired help, everything. It's like free advertising. The last time we did it, we picked up a bunch of new customers."

"If you're sure. I still feel responsible," Gloria said. "I would love to see who all signed up."

"I'm positive and your wish is my command. I'll take a picture of the lists and send them to you in a text message."

"Thanks Dot. You're the best."

"I better get back to work."

The texts arrived moments late, and Gloria's eyes narrowed as she studied the screen. She slipped her reading glasses on but still had trouble reading the small print, so she sent the texts to her email and then settled in at the computer.

The first list was the one from the Montbay County Sheriff's Department. Gloria recognized several of the names, including Pearl Johnson and Minnie Dexter.

Next was the EMS list, which was much shorter.

Last, but not least, was the fire department. Gloria ran her finger along the screen as she studied the names. Owen Belkins, the fire chief, was the first name on the list.

Halfway down the list, she spotted Lauren Dolby's name.

She consulted her notepad for the third name, Tucker McDonald, but his name wasn't on the list. Perhaps he hadn't been at work when the invitation was posted.

Gloria was disappointed, but there was nothing she could do about it, and two out of three wasn't bad.

After perusing the lists, she started a shopping list of items Paul and she would need to spruce up Paul's farm and get it rent ready.

She texted Lucy, asking her to call when she got a chance, and then Gloria and Mally wandered into the front yard where she stopped to inspect Ryan and Tyler's tree fort. She remembered how excited the boys had been the day they built it and how she'd let them spend the night in it while she slept on the porch to keep an eye on them.

Clank. Clank. Gloria shifted her gaze to the road out front and watched as Gus and his tow truck drove by. Hooked to the back of his truck was a hot pink Cadillac with a crumpled front quarter panel and a bent rim. It was Eleanor's car.

Chapter 16

Gloria made a beeline for Paul's workshop. "I'm going to run up to Gus' shop for a minute. He just drove past the house in his wrecker and he was towing Eleanor's pink Cadillac with a crumpled front end."

"Oh no." Paul set his sander on the workbench. "I hate to say it, but it was an accident waiting to happen."

"I'm afraid you're right. I want to make sure Eleanor is okay. I'll be back in a few minutes." Gloria headed back to the house to grab her car keys and purse. She drove to the edge of town where G.S. Towing and Auto, Gus and Beth's towing and repair shop, were located.

Gus was standing next to Eleanor's car when Gloria pulled into the parking lot.

She hopped out of her car and hurried over.

"Hi Gloria. Is Annabelle causing you trouble already?" Gus had given Gloria's car a complete overhaul and, thanks to Gus, she was running like a top.

"No. I saw Eleanor's car on the back of your tow truck and wondered what happened."

"It was only a minor fender bender." Gus lowered the hook, releasing the car. "She miscalculated the distance between the front of her car and a light pole."

"Is she okay?" Gloria asked.

"Yeah. She's a little shaken up, but the only thing wounded is her pride," Gus said. "In her defense, these older cars are tanks. Since the incident occurred on private property, she didn't have to file a police report."

"She didn't want to, did she?"

"Nope. In fact, when I mentioned it, she started to panic," Gus said.

"That's because her driver's license expired years ago," Gloria said.

Gus lifted a brow. "Does she have auto insurance?"

"I have no idea. I guess I need to take her to the Secretary of State to get a new license and make sure she has insurance."

"Someone needs to. Eleanor got lucky this time."

Gloria looked around. "Where is Eleanor?"

"Beth gave her a ride home."

"I'll stop by to visit with her tomorrow," Gloria said. "I don't want to upset her more than she already is, plus the roads are safe until you return her vehicle. How much damage did she do?"

"She bent her axle, ruined the tire and has a dandy ding in the front quarter panel. Eleanor told me to go ahead with the repairs but it's gonna take a few days to get the parts." Gus hooked his thumbs in his front pants pocket. "I'd say her car will be out of commission until Monday at the earliest."

"I'm on it." Gloria patted Gus' arm. "Remember, you didn't hear about her driver's license from me."

Gus made a zipping motion across his mouth. "My lips are sealed."

Gloria thanked him for the information and climbed back in the car. When she arrived home, she parked in the garage and then wandered into the shop where Paul was still sanding the trim boards.

A sawdust haze filled the air and Gloria sneezed. "Do you want some help?"

"Bless you." Paul pushed the safety goggles on top of his head. "Are you offering?"

"Yeah. I mean if you want me to help."

"Sure." Paul handed her a piece of sandpaper. "I'm able to smooth out most of the boards except for the corners." He pointed out the rough edges and Gloria started sanding the corners of the boards.

"How are Eleanor and her car?" Paul asked.

"According to Gus, she miscalculated her distance from a concrete pole in a parking lot. She crumpled her front bumper, ruined a tire and bent her axle. Gus said she's shook up. Beth gave her a ride home but her car is out of commission until early next week, so I'm going to run over there tomorrow morning to talk to her."

"She could've been slapped with a reckless driving charge, driving with an expired license, driving without proof of insurance, which would have set her back a thousand dollars in fines," Paul said.

While they worked, she told Paul she planned to take Eleanor to the Secretary of State to renew her driver's license and make sure she had ample insurance on the vehicle. "I think she's afraid she won't pass the test."

"She'll be in a lot worse shape if she gets in another accident and she's driving around on an expired license," Paul pointed out.

"I know. I'm going to see if I can track down a copy of the driving test, print it off and take it over to her place first thing tomorrow morning."

***

Gloria printed off the driver's information and then began searching the Montbay County Fire Department's website to see if she could find pictures of Fire Chief Owen Belkins, Lauren Dolby and perhaps even Tucker McDonald.

As she searched, Gloria was reminded of how much a person could find out about a complete stranger from looking at their online social page and vowed to go into hers to check her settings.

She clicked on the fire department's website and Chief Belkins' photo first, using the website links to the chief's social media page.

Gloria enlarged the picture and used her cell phone's camera to take a picture of the image. After digging around, she also found Lauren Dolby and Tucker McDonald, repeating the same steps when she found the link to their personal pages.

Her last search was for Vanessa Hines. Gloria quickly located her page. She studied the woman's features. She was even younger than Gloria envisioned. Her short, dark hair framed her face and she was laughing.

She scrolled the screen and stopped on a second picture. In this one, Vanessa was standing on the edge of a dock. She was holding a young girl's hand and they were both smiling.

Gloria double clicked on the picture. The woman was wearing a pair of jogging shorts, a fitted tank top and jogging shoes and Gloria grudgingly admitted the woman was...had been fit and firm.

After she finished scrolling the page, she logged off the computer, grabbed the copy of the driving skills study guide and set it next to her purse.

Paul, who was in the kitchen finishing the last of his morning coffee, pointed at the stack of paper. "You weren't kidding when you said you were going to talk to Eleanor."

"Yes. I'm planning a driving intervention. I love Eleanor and would hate to see anything happen to her or for her to cause an accident."

Paul rinsed his cup and set it in the sink. "So I guess I'm on my own for dinner this evening since you've so generously offered to help Dot host the thank-you spaghetti dinner."

"Yes and don't look at me like that. It won't hurt to get a little insider info on the group who works at the fire department."

Margaret, Lucy, Ruth and Gloria planned to arrive at Dot's at five o'clock to go over their job assignments. "It ends at 7:30 and I'll bring some leftovers home, if there are any."

The dinner started at six. Dot told them the place would fill up fast so they would need all hands on deck to handle everyone arriving at the same time.

Ray and Johnnie were in charge of kitchen duty since the women planned to remain out front and mingle with the responders.

Earlier, Gloria had texted Andrea to ask how she was feeling and offered to drop off some leftover chicken casserole she had in her freezer before heading to Eleanor's place.

She grabbed the casserole and placed it in a plastic grocery bag while Mally waited by the door.

"It looks like someone wants to tag along," Paul said as he reached for the casserole dish.

Gloria patted the pooch's head. "She can visit with Brutus for a few minutes before we head to Eleanor's house."

Paul carried the dish and walked them to the car.

"I should be back before lunch," Gloria said as she took the casserole from Paul.

"I think I might work on the fishing shanty today. The patch I put on last winter was only temporary and there are some large gaps near the floor that need to be sealed." He glanced up at the dark clouds. "But first, I'll move it into the barn in case it starts to rain." Paul leaned down and kissed his wife. "Try to stay out of trouble."

Gloria closed the car door and rolled down the window. "I will, at least until later tonight."

It only took a few minutes to reach the outskirts of town and Gloria passed by Gus' tow shop. Eleanor's pink Cadillac was parked off to the side.

She headed up the hill to Andrea's place and parked behind Andrea's truck.

Mally bolted across the seat and headed for the front door while Gloria brought up the rear. She rang the bell and rapped the doorknocker.

Alice opened the door. "Oh, Miss Gloria. You didn't have to bring food."

"They're just some leftovers." Gloria handed the dish to Alice.

Alice motioned Gloria inside. "I have been busy trying to take care of Andrea and also work at the dog kennel with Marco."

The previous fall, Gloria had met Marco Acosta when she visited his farm. His farm, which also housed a dog kennel, had been in disrepair and after seeing the sad condition of the place, Gloria offered to loan Marco money to make some much-needed repairs and to start *At Your Service,* a dog training and dog kennel service.

Alice, Andrea and her family's former housekeeper, had moved from New York to be near Andrea and began working at the dog kennel. "How is the dog kennel doing?"

"Not so good." Alice frowned. "The dogs, they have been getting sick, one right after another. We lost Romeo, one of the sweetest dogs."

Tears welled up in Alice's eyes. "I don't know what happened. One day, he fine and the next, he so sick. We take him to the vet, Andy Cohen. He say Romeo seem healthy, but maybe he have some sort of virus that is going around."

"I'm sorry Alice." Gloria patted her shoulder.

"We had a family lined up for Romeo. The man, he heartbroken to lose Romeo." Gloria knew what it was like to lose a pet, a family member. Her heart still ached when she thought about Bingo, the family dog the kids had growing up.

Bingo and the children had been playing in the backyard when the pup got away from them. He ran into the road and was struck by a car.

"Hi Gloria." Andrea made her way through the dining room. "I thought Alice was in here talking to herself again." She noted the sad look on Alice's face. "You told her about Romeo."

Alice's lower lip trembled. "Yes. I take this to the kitchen." She carried the casserole out of the room.

Andrea waited until she was gone. "She's torn up about Romeo. Something is going on at the kennel. They've had three dogs come down with similar symptoms and then Romeo died yesterday."

"I hate to hear that." Gloria patted Mally's head. She would be devastated if anything happened to Mally. "Where's Brutus?"

"He's in the backyard. Ever since I put a doggie door in the kitchen, Brutus loves to go in and out."

"Mally, do you want to check out the new doggy door?"

When they reached the kitchen, Mally made a beeline for the doggie door. Gloria peeked out the window as the two dogs greeted each other.

She turned to Andrea. "How are you feeling?"

"Today is a better day. I'm going to try to make it to Dot's tonight but I don't think I can handle kitchen duty."

Gloria squeezed Andrea's hand. "I think you should take it easy and stay home."

"I'm tired of staying home. I'm going stir crazy."

"I try to get her to rest, but she no listen," Alice said.

Mally and Brutus bolted through the doggie door and Mally skidded to a halt near Gloria's feet. When she lifted her head, Gloria noticed a tuft of brown fur.

"What do you have in your mouth?" She loosened the dog's jaw and a baby bunny rabbit fell onto the floor. "Oh dear."

Andrea grabbed Mally and Brutus' collars and led them to the other side of the kitchen.

The baby bunny's paw began to quiver. "It looks like he's still alive. We should take him back outside and try to find his home."

Alice darted to the broom closet, grabbed a broom and dustpan and hurried over. "We must not touch him. I scoop him into the dustpan." She gently swept the small creature into the dustpan and carried him out the back door.

Brutus began to growl. Andrea kept a firm grip on both dogs' collars. "I'll keep an eye on these two."

Alice started on one side of the backyard and Gloria started on the other as they walked the perimeter of the fence. Near the right hand corner of the yard, Gloria spotted a large tree with a hollowed out section near the base. "I think I may have found the nest."

Gloria jogged to the gate and stepped on the other side of the fence.

Alice, who was still carrying the dustpan, met her near the back.

"I found the nest." Alice handed the dustpan and bunny over the top of the fence and Gloria dropped to her knees. She gently placed the edge of the dustpan on the ground and eased the small bunny into the nest. He rolled over and his small ears started to twitch.

"The mother, she over there." Alice pointed to a swath of tall grass.

Gloria backed away from the nest and watched as a rabbit crept toward the nest, all the while keeping one eye on Gloria.

"I'm leaving." She made her way back inside the fence and secured the gate. "The adventurous young one must've snuck through the chain link fence and Mally found him."

Mally, Brutus and Andrea were waiting near the back door. "You found the nest."

"And the mother," Alice said. "We think the little one snuck through the chain link fence."

Gloria walked to the kitchen sink and turned the faucet on. "Are we still on for the Sunday luncheon? I haven't mentioned it to the girls yet. I planned to ask them tonight."

"Yes, we will be there Miss Gloria," Alice said. "I will eat Andrea's share of cake if she doesn't want it."

"Perfect. I can hardly wait." Gloria turned to Andrea. "We're meeting at Dot's at five to go over the game plan."

Andrea gave a thumbs-up. "I'll be there, unless I'm puking again."

"It will be all worth it in the end," Gloria said. She hugged Alice and Andrea and then Mally and she headed to the car. It was time to track down Eleanor.

Chapter 17

During the short ride to Eleanor's house, Gloria mulled over how to approach her friend about the driving test. Should she tell Eleanor she already knew about the fender bender or let Eleanor tell her?

She decided to play it by ear as Mally and she headed up the front steps. She could hear the *thump thump* of hip-hop music as she rang the bell and wondered if Eleanor would even hear it.

The music stopped. Moments later, the door swung open and Eleanor peered out. "Hello Gloria."

"Hi Eleanor. Do you have a minute?"

"I've got two. C'mon in." Eleanor unlocked the screen door and stepped to the side.

"I have Mally with me." Mally slipped inside the house and greeted Eleanor, who leaned forward and patted Mally's head. "Aren't you all pretty today?"

"She just had a bath. Unintentional, of course. Mally found a batch of stinkweed. I think she did it on purpose," Gloria joked.

"A stinker in the stinkweed," Eleanor said. "Let's go get you a doggie treat." Mally and Gloria followed Eleanor into the kitchen where the elderly woman kept a small Tupperware container of doggy treats. She gave one to Mally and then eyed the stack of papers Gloria was holding. "What's that?"

"These are the instructions for the state driving test you need to take." Gloria placed the papers on the corner of the kitchen table.

"I don't..."

Gloria held up a hand. "You do. Where's your car?"

Eleanor cleared her throat.

"It's at Gus' repair shop," Gloria said. "I watched him tow it past my house last night. I noticed a large dent in the front bumper, so I drove down to his shop to find out what happened."

"It was an accident," Eleanor whispered. "I miscalculated the distance between the front of my car and a large concrete pole."

"Of course it was an accident, Eleanor." Gloria softened her tone. "I adore you my dear friend. The last thing I want is to see you get hurt or to hurt someone else."

"But what if I take the test and I can't pass?"

"I'll help you. When your car is out of the shop, we'll brush up on some of the basics. It's nothing to be ashamed of. If I were in your shoes, I would have to do the same thing."

"You'll do that for me?"

"Of course. We'll go over the written part as a refresher and also spend some time driving around."

Eleanor tugged on a stray strand of hair. "It scared the dickens out of me. The front end of my car is so long. At first, I wasn't sure what I hit."

Gloria walked across the kitchen and put an arm around Eleanor's shoulders. "God gave you a mini wake up call, but don't worry. We're going to turn you into the next Mario Andretti, minus the speed, of course."

"Of course." Eleanor's shoulders relaxed. "I'm glad I didn't have to tell you what happened. It was bad enough having to explain it to Gus."

"Gus and Beth care about you, too. We all want you to be as independent, happy and carefree as possible."

"I made some ginger tea. Would you like to try it?"

"Of course." Eleanor poured two cups of tea and they settled in at the table. "Gus said I wouldn't get my car back until Monday. I was going to drive to the dance this weekend."

"Can you hitch a ride with someone else?"

"Doris is planning on going. Maybe I can ride with her. It's Elvis night, you know."

"It sounds exciting." The women chatted about the damage to Eleanor's car and then Eleanor told her the Pilates class was going gangbusters, how she was tossing around the idea of moving it out of her place and into the VFW hall. "Would you like to check it out?"

"When is it?" Gloria hadn't participated in a structured exercise class in years.

"We're meeting every Monday and Wednesday morning at nine. There's also an evening class but I'm sure you would rather be home with Paul."

"How about if I give it a try next Monday," Gloria said.

"Wear something comfortable. Yoga pants work best." Eleanor rattled off a list of other items including a tank top, tennis shoes and a foam mat.

"And some ibuprofen," Gloria said.

"You'll only be sore for the first couple of weeks." Eleanor slid a plate of chocolate chip cookies across the table. "Would you like a cookie? I made these yesterday."

"Thanks. Chocolate chip cookies are one of my favorites." Gloria grabbed a cookie and took a big bite.

The cookie was dry and a big chunk clung to the roof of Gloria's mouth. "What is this?" she asked as bits of the crumbled cookie fell from her mouth. She cupped her hand under her chin.

"Almond chickpea cookies made with vegan chocolate chips. The recipe is 100% vegan, gluten-free and preservative-free. You can even eat the dough right out of the bowl." Eleanor broke off a piece of her cookie and popped it into her mouth. "They're addicting. I could sit here and eat the whole plate."

Not wanting to hurt Eleanor's feelings, Gloria finished chewing the cookie, mixing it with her tea before swallowing. "I don't believe I've ever had an almond chickpea chocolate chip cookie."

Gloria gulped her tea, forcing the dry cookie down her throat. "Mally and I should head home. We have some work to do around the house before I help out at the first responder's spaghetti dinner down at Dot's later."

Eleanor accompanied Gloria and Mally to the front door. "That's so nice of Dot to host a free meal. That woman has a heart of gold."

"Yes, Dot is a wonderful person," Gloria agreed. She thanked Eleanor for the tea and cookie and then promised she would come by Monday for the Pilates class. "After the class, we can go over the driving test questions and also take a drive around town."

Eleanor followed Gloria and Mally out onto the front porch. "I've been thinking about Judith Arnett's incident. What if someone tried to run her over on purpose? I'm tempted to go out and buy myself a handgun."

Gloria's eyes widened. If Eleanor's shooting skills were anything close to her driving skills, there was cause for concern. She said the first thing that popped into her head. "Before you buy a gun, why don't we see if Lucy can give you a few pointers on handling one?"

"Wouldn't hurt to have a refresher," Eleanor agreed. "Years ago, I used to go deer hunting with Matthew."

Gloria made a mental note to get with Lucy as soon as possible. Once Eleanor got something stuck in her head, she moved full steam ahead. It was only a couple of weeks ago that she was talking about taking her car out of storage.

The thought of a pistol-packing Eleanor sent a chill down Gloria's spine. "After the Pilates class, we can go over the written part of the driving test and take our first driving lesson to Lucy's place to look at her guns."

Project Eleanor was turning into a full-time job!

Gloria thanked her again for the tea and cookie before Mally and she climbed into the car. "I might have to start taking some of Rose's special elixir so I can keep up with Eleanor."

Back at the house, Gloria worked on her list for the girls' special luncheon. She decided to make some pink cupcakes and blue cupcakes as a clue. Her original plan was to have an afternoon tea and then remembered Andrea telling her just the thought of tuna made her sick, so she decided to host a Sunday brunch instead.

She could throw together a baked casserole the night before and stick it in the fridge. The breakfast bombs would be a perfect side and easy to make.

Gloria finished the list by adding buttermilk mini stack pancakes, bacon and the cupcakes for dessert.

Next, she jotted down a grocery list for the items she would need to purchase and then wandered out to the barn.

Ding. Ding. Gloria covered her ears and waited for the sound of clanging metal to stop. "Hello?"

Paul emerged from the shanty. "How did it go with Eleanor?"

"Good. I think the fender bender shook her up and she realizes she needs a little more practice behind the wheel."

Paul set his hammer on the floor. "Did you check on Andrea?"

"Yes. She's feeling better. I think she's going stir crazy, so she plans to join us this evening at Dot's to help out, if she's not throwing up again."

Gloria stepped into the barn. "I have no idea what to have for lunch so I was thinking of running to Meijer to pick up the groceries for the Sunday brunch and maybe grab a rotisserie chicken to munch on. That way, you'll have leftovers in case we run out of spaghetti at Dot's."

"Do you want me to go with you?"

"No. I can go by myself. Can you keep an eye on Mally while I'm gone?"

Paul promised he would and Gloria headed back out. She decided to take a spin through town, past the flea market.

Gloria had met the owner, Peter Giese, not long ago when she chased after a small dog who had wandered into one of his buildings. She caught a glimpse of his large home, beyond the flea market grounds atop a large hill.

Rumor around town was that Giese was a doomsday prepper and his property was booby-trapped. She turned the corner, drove past Bea McQueen's place and around the next block.

She thought about stopping by Judith's place to check on her but kept going instead. Gloria turned onto Vanessa's tree-lined street and slowed as she approached the house.

The curtains were still closed. Gloria's eyes traveled to the third story windows and she shivered. The half-moon eyes were staring back at her.

She pulled off the street and shifted into park before reaching for the door handle and slipping out of the car. The crime scene tape was long gone. The Buick sedan was still in the drive.

Gloria slowly wandered into the backyard and then circled around to the other the side of the house. *Why had Vanessa purchased flowers for herself and stuck Paul's name on the card?*

The woman knew Gloria planned to stop by that morning. Had she purchased them to make Gloria jealous? She thought of Deputy Bowman's statement that Vanessa had her share of enemies.

Gloria hoped the spaghetti dinner would turn up some new clues. Even if the woman's co-workers hadn't been involved in her death, surely someone who worked with Vanessa would be able to fill them in on the timeline leading up to her death.

She thought of Doris Tipple, Eleanor's friend, who was a distant relative of Vanessa's. Doris lived in the area. Was there bad blood between them?

Gloria gingerly tiptoed to the side yard. A tall hedge ran from the front corner of the property all the way to the back while six-foot, dog-eared fence panels ran along the back of the property and up the other side.

She began to make her way to the front yard when something inside one of the basement window wells caught her eye. Gloria bent down to pick it up.

"Hey! What are you doing?"

Chapter 18

Gloria stumbled backward, her arms flailing in the air. "Lucy Carlson. You're going to give me a heart attack."

"Sorry. I followed you through town, past the flea market and then watched you pull in here so I thought I'd see how your investigation is going."

"It isn't," Gloria said glumly. "I hope we'll be able to glean some clues during the dinner at Dot's this evening. If not, I'm out of luck."

"What's that?" Lucy pointed at the object Gloria noticed before Lucy scared the daylights out of her.

Gloria bent down and picked it up. "It's a cigarette butt. Marlboro." She rolled the brown butt between her fingers. "Vanessa's cousin,

Doris, told Eleanor that Vanessa was a health nut, almost to the point of obsession."

"Maybe she was a closet smoker," Lucy said. "Everyone has a vice."

"True. You got something I can put this in?"

"A Kleenex." Lucy reached inside her purse and pulled out a tissue. "Don't worry. I haven't used it yet."

Gloria wrinkled her nose. "I hope not." She carefully wrapped the butt in the tissue. "Andrea plans to help out at Dot's tonight."

"How is she feeling?"

"Better. Which reminds me, I want to have a Sunday brunch at my place, after church but before visiting the shut-ins. I was thinking around 1:00."

"Sunday brunch?" Lucy asked. "What's the occasion?"

"Does there have to be a special occasion? Can't I ask all of my closest friends to come over for food and fellowship?"

"Of course. Do you want me to bring something?"

Gloria rattled off her planned menu. "You can bring orange juice and your preferred creamy sweetener. How's it going with cutting back on sweets?"

"It's torture." Lucy sighed heavily. "I love them so much. Maybe I can bring a cream cheese coffee cake. I'll watch everyone eat it."

"That's not fair," Gloria said as they walked to the front yard. "I'm having cupcakes for dessert, the fancy kind with sprinkles on top."

Bea McQueen drove by in her MINI Cooper; she slowed and stared before waving and continuing down the road.

"She's gonna throw her neck out of joint," Lucy joked.

"Yeah. I'm sure half the town will soon know we were parked in front of Vanessa's place." Gloria walked around the back of her car and opened the driver's side door. "I'll see you at five at Dot's?"

"With bells on," Lucy said.

Gloria drove to Meijer and ended up spending more time and money than she planned. She returned home with not only a rotisserie chicken, but also chicken tenders, a half-pound of baked beans and the deli's baked macaroni and cheese.

While Gloria and Paul ate lunch, she asked her husband about the investigation. "Have you heard anything else on Vanessa's autopsy?"

"They're expecting the results back later today," Paul said. "One of the guys told me he would give me a call. They also had a few more people they planned to question based on Vanessa's cell phone log."

Gloria pulled the tissue out of her pocket and unrolled it, exposing the cigarette butt.

"Don't tell me you've taken up smoking," Paul joked.

"No. I found this in a window well at Vanessa's place." Gloria didn't know if Vanessa smoked, but she had a hunch that Eleanor's friend, Vanessa's distant relative, would know. "I'm not sure if this is a clue or if it belonged to one of the investigators."

"I'm sure you'll figure it out. I'm going to finish working on the shanty." Paul kissed his wife's forehead. "This goes without saying, but you shouldn't be wandering around Vanessa's place."

"You're right. It was kind of a spur-of-the-moment decision." She waited until Paul was outside before calling Eleanor and asking her if she could call Doris, to find out if Vanessa was a smoker.

"I planned to call her anyways, to see if I can hitch a ride to the dance Saturday. I'll call you right back."

True to her word, Eleanor called Gloria back within the hour. "I talked to Doris and she said Vanessa hated cigarette smoke."

Gloria thanked her for the information and told her she would see her on Monday.

When five o'clock rolled around, Gloria stopped by the barn to tell Paul she was leaving and promised him she would try to stay out of trouble.

How much trouble could she get into? Dot's Restaurant would be full of police officers, not to mention firefighters.

***

Gloria stepped inside Dot's empty restaurant and headed to the back where she found Andrea, Lucy, Ruth, Rose and Dot gathered around the kitchen island. "Margaret isn't here yet?"

"Nope." Lucy shook her head. "She called me earlier to tell me she had to run an errand in

Green Springs and said she might be a few minutes late."

"I made some fresh coffee." Dot pointed at the coffee machines. The women each poured a cup of coffee and headed to the large, center table in the front.

They chatted for a few moments, waiting for Margaret to arrive when a bright red car, zoomed into an empty parking spot out front.

Gloria's eyes narrowed. "Is that Margaret?"

"She bought a new car?" Andrea said.

"She didn't say anything about buying a new car. Let's check it out." Lucy sprang from her chair.

The women gathered on the sidewalk in front of the restaurant and watched as Margaret eased out of the car. "Well?"

"You traded in your SUV?" Dot asked.

"Not yet. I'm test driving this Tesla. What do you think?"

"A Tesla?" Rose shook her head.

"It's eco-friendly and can travel up to 295 miles on a single charge. They have a seven-seater SUV, but I thought I'd test drive the car first. Check this out." Margaret clicked the key fob and the back doors popped out and slowly began to rise.

"It looks like a big red bird getting ready to take flight," Dot teased.

Margaret shot her a dark look. "It reminds me of a DeLorean."

Gloria peered inside. "It reminds me of a space ship. Check out the control panel."

"It took the sales guy a little while to show me all the bells and whistles."

Lucy leaned in and tapped a button on the dashboard. "What does this do?"

"Don't touch that." Margaret slapped her hand. "I don't know. I'm still trying to figure everything out."

Ruth, who hadn't said a word, slowly circled the vehicle. "I've been admiring these for a while now. If I didn't have my van, I'd probably look into buying the SUV model."

"And get rid of your van?" Gloria was surprised.

Ruth's van was loaded with cameras and surveillance equipment. She'd volunteered to use her vehicle to test a special bulletproof coating.

Lucy had been itching to fire a few rounds at Ruth's van, but it hadn't been necessary. They'd found out the old-fashioned way that the protective coating worked...by being shot at during two separate investigations.

"There's no way I would get rid of it now," Ruth said. "I was saying if I totaled my van, I might think about getting one of these babies."

"Bite your tongue," Dot scolded.

"How fast does she go?" Ruth asked.

"Zero to sixty in 3.5 seconds. The SUV does zero to sixty in 2.5 seconds. The sales guy almost gave me a heart attack showing me how fast it would go."

"I feel the need for speed," Lucy teased.

"You won't be feeling it in this car with me behind the wheel," Margaret said. "Anyhoo, I have to return it tomorrow."

A customer approached the restaurant entrance and Dot hurried over, explaining the restaurant was closed for a special event. "We better get back inside."

Margaret closed the falcon wing doors and dropped the keys into her purse.

"Can you take me for a spin after the dinner?" Ruth whispered.

"Yes," Margaret nodded. "A *slow* spin."

Dot waited until they were all inside before locking the door behind them.

The women returned to the table and Gloria rubbed her hands together. "So what's the game plan?"

"Based on past experience, we'll get a full onslaught when we open the doors at six," Dot said. "So we'll have to be ready to hit the ground running."

Andrea offered to make the rounds with beverages and to take care of special requests. Dot put Gloria and Lucy in charge of bussing tables.

Since they planned to serve the food buffet style, Dot asked Margaret to make sure they didn't run out of garlic bread, salad mix or the spaghetti and meatballs.

Dot and Rose would be in charge of overseeing the entire dining room to make sure all of the guests were taken care of.

"I hoped to make my rounds, too," Gloria said. "I have photos of the suspects." She pulled her cell phone from her purse, switched it on, opened her picture app and clicked on the picture of Fire Chief Owen Belkins.

"Where did you get the pictures?" Andrea asked.

"The internet. Social media. We should all be mindful of what we post on the internet." Gloria handed the phone to Andrea, who studied the pictures and then passed the phone to Lucy, who was on her other side.

The pictures made their rounds around the table. While the others studied the pictures, Margaret and Lucy filled them in on their visit to the fire station and their theories.

"We should grab a quick bite to eat before the mad rush," Rose said. "I made some tuna salad and a fresh batch of creamy bacon and potato salad." She abruptly stood. "I'll go get the food."

Andrea made a small gurgling noise and covered her mouth. "I'm...not hungry. I think I'll run down to the hardware store to chat with

Brian for a minute while you eat." She bolted from the table and jogged to the door.

"What a shame. I made the sandwiches especially for Andrea," Rose said. "I thought she loved my tuna fish sandwiches."

"Maybe she's full," Dot said. "We'll send some home with her later."

"Speaking of home, I'm inviting all of you to a Sunday bruncheon at my place at 1:00 this Sunday," Gloria said.

"A Sunday bruncheon?" Margaret asked.

"Well, it's not brunch and it's not lunch so I'm calling it a bruncheon," Gloria explained. "We rarely get together to just hang out and I have some recipes I want to try out on you."

"I'll be there," Dot said.

"Me too," Rose chimed in.

All of the women assured Gloria they would be there.

Dot stood. "I'll go grab our food."

"No." Gloria held out her hand. "You sit. I'll go get the food."

"Me too." Lucy shoved her chair back. "It's the least we can do."

"I'll supervise." Rose followed Gloria and Lucy to the kitchen. "Are you sure Andrea is okay? She's been feelin' under the weather a lot lately. I've got the perfect peppermint potion that might cure whatever's ailing her."

"I think she'll be fine." Gloria patted Rose's arm. "Mother hen Rose. You and Dot are a lot alike. Maybe that's why you get along so well."

Lucy carried the sandwiches, Gloria carried the potato salad and Rose grabbed a stack of dinner plates.

"Before I forget, Paul took me to Garfield's the other night for dinner. They put our leftovers in an eco-friendly to-go container. According to the server, the container is 100% biodegradable and compostable. I cleaned it up and brought it with me to show both you and Dot. I left it on top of the pass-through counter."

"Thanks Gloria. We've been lookin' for something more environmentally friendly."

The women ate their food and discussed the possible suspects. Gloria was leaning toward either the co-worker, Lauren, or the ex in jail. "Motive and opportunity. Lauren's motive would be revenge and the ex's would be revenge."

"Both of them knew Vanessa had moved to a new town and probably hadn't met many of her neighbors so a strange car in the drive wouldn't look suspicious."

"We can't talk to Vanessa's ex, but we can certainly try to get a feel for the others." Dot glanced at her watch. "We better finish up. It's almost showtime."

Chapter 19

Andrea returned shortly before six, after the others had finished cleaning up, and she helped set the buffet and the tables.

Rose hurried over when she spotted Andrea near the front of the restaurant. She pressed a small vial into her hand. "I'm worried about you dear. You're skinny as a rail, like you stopped eatin', so I'm givin' you this vial of peppermint and lovage. Now don't worry about the weird name. It's a mixture of parsley, celery, aniseed and curry all rolled up into one. You may have to plug your nose cuz it's kinda stinky but it'll work wonders."

"Thank you Rose. You're so sweet." Andrea gently hugged the robust woman. "I'll go put it in my purse."

Gloria caught the tail end of the conversation. "Are there any side effects?"

Andrea chuckled. "I guess I should've asked that."

Rose adjusted her apron. "Nothin' worth worryin' about. Gives you some bad gas, but there are warnin' signs, a rumblin' from down under if you know what I mean, so you be sure to clear the room before it lets loose."

"Thanks for the warning, Rose. Let's uh, not mention the potion to Alice," Andrea said. "She's been mixing her own concoctions for me, too."

The women wrapped up their dinner preparations at six on the dot and the guests started pouring in.

Gloria was proud to be able to serve those who put their lives on the line every single day to protect, serve and keep Montbay County safe.

She thanked each one she stopped to talk to and they thanked her in return for the delicious meal.

Gloria had only a few fleeting chances to chat with the guests seated at Lauren Dolby's table. She was thrilled when she spotted Tucker McDonald, as well.

Fire Chief Belkins sat with Captain Davies, Paul's former boss. There were a few other familiar faces and Gloria stopped once to chat with them briefly.

Despite her best efforts, there wasn't enough time to eavesdrop on conversations or pick up on anything that might be a clue.

Dot and Rose were in their element as they worked the room.

Margaret did an outstanding job of making sure they didn't run out of food, and when Dot brought out the dessert, a large chocolate sheet cake, Gloria knew the night had been a resounding success, even if she hadn't been able to glean any clues from the suspects.

Rose, Dot, Lucy and Gloria hovered near the back while Andrea, Margaret and Ruth cut the cake and carried dessert plates to each of the tables. "Were you able to find out anything?"

"Yes, ma'am." Rose nodded. "Miss Lauren Dolby can put away some food."

Gloria's eyes drifted to Lauren's table. She watched as Lauren shook her head when Andrea offered her cake. After Andrea walked away, Lauren slid her chair back and walked outside.

She stood in front of the big picture window and Gloria watched as she lit a cigarette and began puffing on it.

"Do you see that?" Lucy whispered. "Lauren Dolby smokes."

After she finished her cigarette, she dropped the butt on the sidewalk and stepped back inside.

"I'm going to grab the cigarette butt." Lucy passed by the woman as she walked out of the restaurant.

Gloria hurried over to distract Lauren and to give Lucy time to collect the cigarette butt. Her heart skipped a beat when she recognized the man seated next to Lauren. "How was your meal?"

"Delicious," Lauren said. "I loved the spaghetti and meatballs as much as the chicken and dumplings from last time."

"Wonderful," Gloria said. "I'm happy to hear you enjoyed your dinner."

Lucy stepped back inside and joined Gloria at the table. She gave her a small shake of the head.

"Hello." Lauren shifted in her seat and gazed at Lucy. "I remember you from the other day."

"My friend, Margaret, and I dropped off the flyer for the dinner and also for my recent property listing," Lucy said. "Has anyone shown an interest in the property?"

The man seated next to Lauren spoke. "This is the lady who owns the renovated farm posted on our bulletin board?"

"Yes, Tucker." Lauren smiled. "It looks like a nice place. Maybe we should take a look at it," she hinted.

"Maybe," Tucker replied.

"Did you guys make it over to Kips Bar for happy hour before coming here?" Lucy asked.

"We did." Lauren nodded. "It's a decent little bar. I'm surprised by how much Belhaven has to offer residents."

"We love our little town." Lucy excused herself and then hurried to the back.

The diners thanked Gloria again and she made her way to the kitchen to help with the cleanup. Soon, the guests started to leave, but not before stopping by to thank Dot, Rose, Ray and Johnnie, who stood near the door.

She watched as Lauren and Tucker exited the restaurant. They climbed into a four-wheel drive truck and backed out of their parking spot before roaring off.

Gloria's heart skipped a beat as she watched them drive off. She hurried to Ruth. "Can you call Judith and ask her where she was struck and if she has any idea the type of vehicle that struck her?"

"Of course." Ruth stepped into the back. When she returned, she tracked down Gloria, who was clearing tables. "She's not certain, but she thinks it was a dark-colored truck and she was struck near the top of her shoulder. I think I mentioned that before. Why?"

"Because I think I know who hit Judith and maybe even killed Vanessa," Gloria said and then motioned Lucy over. "What did you find out about the cigarette that Lauren was smoking?"

"The butt you found in Vanessa's window well had a brown end and said Marlboro. The one that Lauren smoked was white."

"I'll be right back." Gloria hurried out the front door and made her way to Kip's Bar and Grill. When she returned she was grinning from ear-to-ear. "I might be onto something. I can't confirm it until I check out one more thing."

The group cleaned the kitchen, loaded the dishwashers and finished putting everything away. By the time everything was back in order, Gloria's feet hurt and her back ached, but she was proud to have helped.

There were plenty of leftovers, so Gloria grabbed enough for both her and Paul. "Before I forget." She handed Dot the eco-friendly to-go container she'd gotten from Garfield's.

"Thanks." Dot studied the container. "This is exactly what we've been looking for. It even lists the manufacturer."

"I think I'm going to head home," Andrea said and Gloria noticed she was a little pale. "Get some rest."

"I will," Andrea said.

After Andrea left, Margaret hugged Dot and then Rose. "I'm going to head out, too, if you don't need me anymore."

"Thanks Margaret," Dot said. "I appreciate the help." She gazed at her circle of friends. "All of your help."

The rest of the friends said their good-byes to Dot, Rose, Ray and Johnnie.

Ruth followed Margaret out onto the sidewalk. "Maybe you can take me for a spin in the car now?" she asked hopefully.

"Sure," Margaret said. "Anyone else want to go?"

"I'm whupped," Gloria said. "If you buy one, I'll take a ride."

"Me too," Lucy chimed in.

"I guess it's just the two of us." Margaret unlocked the car doors and Ruth climbed into the passenger seat while Margaret slid behind the wheel.

Ruth grinned from ear-to-ear and gave them a thumbs-up.

Gloria and Lucy watched as they eased out onto the street. "You managed to help bring Margaret back around with the reno project. I was worried about her," Gloria said.

"She needed a new purpose in life." Lucy waved as they sped off. "We all need a purpose in life."

"And you helped her find it." Gloria linked arms with Lucy and they strolled across the street to the post office where they'd parked their vehicles. "I haven't had time to fill you in on Eleanor's antics. I was wondering if she and I could stop by Monday afternoon and you can show her your gun collection; maybe give her a few pointers on shooting a gun."

Lucy stopped abruptly. "Do you think it's wise for Eleanor to own a gun? She can't even see her car's dashboard."

"I don't, but Eleanor does," Gloria said. "I was hoping you could talk her out of it."

"So what about your mysterious clues? Care to fill me in?"

"Not yet. I want to check something out first." When they reached their vehicles, Gloria leaned against her driver's side door. "I think it's just a matter of putting all of the puzzle pieces in place."

"I'm sure you'll figure it out." Lucy set her bag of food on the passenger seat and eased into her jeep. She nodded toward Dot's Restaurant. "I'm concerned about Andrea. She's been sick a lot lately. Did you see her bolt when Rose said we were having tuna salad sandwiches for dinner? I thought she was going to throw up."

"I'm sure Andrea will be okay."

Gloria told Lucy good-bye and wearily climbed into her car. There was one more stop to make. She drove to the other side of town, toward Vanessa's place.

Chapter 20

Gloria slowly drove past Vanessa's house. When she reached the end of the block, she turned onto the next street and parked off to the side.

She exited her car and walked to the corner where she was able to see a portion of the deceased woman's driveway. Vanessa had told Sally Keane she thought someone had followed her home, but she couldn't tell the type of vehicle because the headlights shined in the rearview mirror.

Cars sometimes blinded Gloria at night while she was driving, but more often than not, truck lights were the culprits, especially when following behind a car...say a Buick sedan like Vanessa's car.

According to Ruth, Judith was struck in the upper part of her shoulder, near the top, so the mirrors on the vehicle sat higher, which meant it was more than likely an SUV...or a truck. Like the truck Tucker McDonald drove.

Gloria suspected that Vanessa and Lauren had been involved in some sort of altercation. Then when she found the cigarette butt on Vanessa's property and saw Lauren smoking on the sidewalk, she thought she had Vanessa's attacker, but Lucy said it wasn't the same type of cigarette.

A trip to Kip's Bar and Grill confirmed the fact. Lauren had been smoking Virginia Slim cigarettes. Kip even showed Gloria the ashtray Lauren and Tucker had been using. There were white cigarette butts, lined with lipstick. There were also brown Marlboro cigarette butts in the ashtray.

Gloria continued walking until she caught a glimpse of Judith's driveway and front door. She slowly shifted her gaze. If Judith stood at the end of her driveway or on her front stoop, she had a clear view of Vanessa's driveway.

Tall hedges and a fence obscured the view from the neighbors beside and behind Vanessa's property, but the neighbors across the street had an unobstructed view.

Judith mentioned she'd started walking around the neighborhood in the early evening. What if Judith had walked by Vanessa's place and seen something...or *someone*?

She shifted her gaze, her eyes traveling to the second story windows where she caught a small movement from one of the windows. Gloria took a step closer. One of the windows was open and a lace curtain fluttered.

Gloria kept one eye on the open window as she fumbled around inside her purse. She dialed Ruth's cell phone number.

"Whoee!" Ruth shrieked into the phone. "Hi Gloria."

"Hi Ruth. I take it you're enjoying the Tesla."

"This baby rockets down the road."

"Where are you rocketing to now?"

"We're on the curves right outside of town. What's up?"

"Can you ask Margaret to swing by Elm Street? I parked on the side street, but I'm standing in front of Vanessa Hines' place on the sidewalk across the street."

"Will do." Ruth told her they would be there soon before hanging up the phone.

Gloria's next call was to Paul.

"I was starting to worry. Are you on your way home?"

"No. I'm standing in front of Vanessa's house," Gloria said. "I'm waiting for Ruth and Margaret."

"You're wasting your time," Paul said. "I talked to one of the investigators. They're ruling Vanessa's death as accidental. They found bruises on her body, consistent with a fall and after examining the premises, they concluded she must have lost her footing and accidentally fell down her basement stairs."

"I think they're wrong," Gloria said. "What about Judith Arnett's hit and run?"

"They could be totally unrelated," Paul said. "People panic and leave accident scenes all of the time."

"I think someone pushed Vanessa down her basement stairs and that someone was Tucker McDonald. My theory is, he was harassing Vanessa, following her home. Tucker lied to Lauren, claiming Vanessa was after him when it was really the other way around."

Gloria told her husband she was standing in front of Vanessa's house and planned to dig through her garbage but noticed that one of the upstairs windows was open. "The authorities need to check the place, including the attic."

"Now?" Paul interrupted Gloria's thoughts.

"Now would be optimal. Do you think the investigators still have a valid search warrant?" Gloria asked.

"It's valid for ten days from the date of issuance and can hold up in court if they have a valid reason for entering the property under the guise of probable cause." Paul groaned. "I'll give them a call, but they're not going to be happy if I send them on a wild goose chase."

"It's not a wild goose chase. I'm onto something. I can feel it in my bones." Gloria thanked Paul and promised him she would stay put and let the authorities handle it. She disconnected the line as the roar of an automobile engine filled the air.

Gloria caught a glimpse of a car zip down the side street. It was Margaret and Ruth. She jogged to her car and waited while Margaret parked the Tesla behind Annabelle.

Ruth jumped out. "Man. This is one awesome vehicle."

Margaret exited the car and met Gloria on the sidewalk. "Ruth is in love with the Tesla."

"I'm going to get one when my van is paid for," Ruth said. "So what's up?"

Gloria briefly explained her theory and the open window.

"You think this Tucker guy is inside the house?"

"Maybe."

"How does this connect to Judith's hit and run?" Margaret asked.

"The other night, Judith told Ruth and me that she's walking around the neighborhood in the evenings," Gloria said. "I think Judith may have seen someone in or around Vanessa's home. Perhaps it was McDonald, lurking in the yard and he followed her back to her place."

"So McDonald tried to take Judith out," Ruth said. "It's a stretch."

"Think about it, the cigarette butt, the fact that Vanessa claimed McDonald was after her. Someone with tall headlights followed her home," Gloria said.

"Maybe the house killed Vanessa. It reminds me of the Amityville Horror house," Margaret said. "It's probably haunted and the ghost wanted Vanessa out."

An unmarked four-door sedan turned onto the street. "I bet that's the investigator," Gloria said.

The women hurried down the sidewalk and hovered across the street from Vanessa's place, watching as the car pulled in behind Vanessa's Buick.

Two men exited the car and disappeared behind the back of the house. The women watched as bright lights illuminated the interior of the house.

Gloria caught a flash of light peeking out from the top of the drawn curtains. "Don't forget to check the second story, the attic and the basement," Gloria whispered.

Moments later, lights flickered in the open window and the window slammed shut. The investigators exited the home and climbed into their car.

"Uh-oh. It appears that my hunch was wrong. Paul is gonna kill me," Gloria clasped her hands. "Ruth, you said Judith mentioned she was wearing a special bracelet when she was hit, and that the bracelet broke."

"Yep," Ruth nodded. "She's still ticked off about it."

"I know I've already said this once and at the risk of sounding like a broken record, I think I might be onto something," Gloria said.

Chapter 21

Gloria darted from the counter, to the refrigerator, to the stove. The timer chimed and she pulled the golden brown breakfast bombs from the oven. She brushed melted butter on top before sprinkling poppy seeds on the top of each one. "Perfect."

Next, she stacked the fried bacon on a large plate before pulling a tray of fresh fruit from the refrigerator.

Paul, who had jumped in to help his harried wife finish the last minute preparations for the girls' "bruncheon," flipped the last pancake before adding it to the towering stack. "All of this food is making me hungry."

"Would you like to join us?" Gloria asked.

"No. I think I'll take a plate of goodies to my workshop and listen to the football game instead. You girls enjoy yourselves." He placed the platter of pancakes in the center of the table.

"Thank you for helping me," Gloria said. She watched as Paul filled his plate with a small stack of pancakes, some crispy bacon, two of the breakfast bombs and an array of fruit. He filled a travel mug with coffee and juggled the coffee and plate of food as he made his way to the porch door.

"Don't you want a cupcake?" Gloria asked as she opened the door.

"Yes. I almost forgot."

She hurried to the pantry, gingerly pulled a blue cupcake from the tiered arrangement and carefully placed it on the edge of his plate before bouncing up on her tiptoes to kiss his cheek. "I love you. Have I ever told you that you're the best husband in the world?"

"Yes, but I never get tired of hearing it."

Gloria held the door for him and then ran to the bathroom to change her blouse and spritz some perfume on her wrists before heading back to the kitchen.

Margaret and her new Tesla were the first to arrive. Ruth pulled in behind her, followed by Lucy. Dot and Rose were next. She ushered them all inside. "We're waiting on Alice and Andrea."

She poured cups of coffee from a large carafe Dot brought with her. "I figured your poor little pot couldn't keep up with this bunch." She sniffed the air appreciatively. "Something smells delicious."

"Fried bacon," Ruth said. "What could be better?"

"It could be my breakfast bombs," Gloria said. She explained the dish was a mixture of scrambled eggs, cheese, more bacon and chives she placed inside biscuit dough and then baked them in the oven.

"You're making me hungry," Margaret groaned.

"Good. We have plenty of food. Andrea and Alice are here." Gloria hurried to the door and waited for the women on the porch. "Last, but not least," she teased as she hugged Alice and then Andrea.

"I'm nervous," Andrea whispered.

"As a jumping bean," Alice added.

"It's going to be fun." Gloria held the door and followed the women inside.

The kitchen filled with excited chatter. Finally, Gloria grew impatient and began clapping her hands. "We can visit after we eat. I don't want the food to get cold."

She stood off to the side as the women filled their plates, oohing and aahing over the breakfast bombs. Gloria was the last to fill her plate with food and she took the empty seat, in between Andrea and Dot. "Let's pray."

The room grew quiet and the women bowed their heads. "Dear Lord. Thank you for this day. We pray, Lord, that you bless this food to our bodies. Thank you for all of my wonderful friends gathered around this table. I pray for each and every one of them. Thank you most of all for our Savior, Jesus Christ."

"Amen," the women echoed.

Gloria sipped her coffee, eyeing her friends gathered at the table and she began to tear up. She wished she could hold onto this moment, long enough to melt it into her heart.

They were growing older now. Their kids were grown and even their grandchildren were growing up.

Life had changed in the small town of Belhaven over the past few years, some of the changes for the better, like Gloria and Paul's marriage, not to mention Andrea and Brian's marriage. There were also new friends who joined them at the table...Alice and Rose.

God had truly blessed Gloria...blessed them all.

After they finished eating, they made quick work of loading the dishwasher and then refilled their coffee cups.

"Chalk another one up for Gloria and her super sleuthing," Lucy teased.

"Start from the beginning," Ruth said. "Alice wasn't in the loop for some of the mystery."

"I'll start with the flowers. As you know, the investigators found a vase of flowers on Vanessa's table with a card that said they were from Paul. Paul was able to track down the florist who confirmed Vanessa purchased the flowers herself the day before Mally found her in her basement."

"So she knew you were coming Sunday for a Garden Girls visit and was going to try to make you jealous," Ruth said.

"And possibly cause trouble with Paul," Rose added.

"Yes. From the get go, it looked bad. I found, I mean *Mally* found Vanessa's body at the bottom of the stairs. The investigators discovered the flowers, which were supposedly from Paul. To top it all off, Vanessa's cell phone was near her body and the last number she called was mine."

She went on to tell her friends despite a number of people who may have had a motive for getting into a physical altercation with Vanessa, there were no other clues.

"Except for the cigarette butt we found in Vanessa's window well," Lucy pointed out.

"True. It was a clue but they didn't match the brand that Lauren smoked," Gloria said. "Vanessa stopped by the Quik Stop and told Sally Keane she suspected someone had been inside her home."

"A stalker," Lucy said.

Gloria continued. "Brian corroborated the story when Vanessa stopped by *Nails and Knobs* to purchase new door and window locks. Judith's hit and run threw me off, but I suspected they were somehow connected. Then I remembered how Judith mentioned she enjoyed Eleanor's Pilates classes and had even started walking around town at night, which made me wonder if the culprit thought Judith may have spotted him or her."

"Lurking around Vanessa's property," Andrea said.

"Correct," Gloria said. "Back to the cigarette butt. Vanessa was a health nut and hated cigarette smoke. It didn't belong to Lauren. I knew that Lauren and Tucker had stopped by Kip's before heading to Dot's for dinner. Lauren smoked. What if Tucker smoked, too?"

She continued. "Almost everyone who stops by Kip's is a regular, so when Lauren and Tucker showed up, Kip remembered them and where they sat. Luckily, he hadn't even emptied their ashtray yet. There were two kinds of cigarette butts in the ashtray…white ones with lipstick prints and Marlboros with brown tips, similar to the one we found in Vanessa's window well."

"How did you tie Tucker and Judith's incident?" Rose said. "That's downright frightening."

"Ruth said Judith mentioned hearing the roar of an engine before seeing the vehicle's headlights coming right toward her. She also said the vehicle's mirror clipped her at the top of her shoulder. It had to be a taller vehicle, an SUV or a pick-up truck. When I watched Lauren and Tucker leave the restaurant and climb into a four-wheel drive truck, I thought I might be onto something."

"So you think Tucker showed up or Vanessa caught him on her property, they got into some sort of altercation and he pushed her down the stairs, causing her to hit her head," Lucy said.

"Why wouldn't she have just called the police on him when she found him in her house?" Margaret said.

"My theory is that she tried. I think that's why her cell phone was found near her body." Gloria told them she contacted Detective Green and shared with him what she knew. He visited Judith and showed her a picture of a truck, similar to McDonald's truck and she was almost certain it was like the one that hit her.

"Tucker, of course, denied it," Gloria said, "until Detective Green asked to take a look at his vehicle and the passenger side mirror, where the detective found a large scratch on the back."

Ruth's eyes widened. "Judith's bracelet!"

"Yep." Gloria nodded triumphantly. "McDonald confessed to striking Judith and after some intense questioning, he also confessed to an obsession with Vanessa. He was using Lauren to try to make Vanessa jealous."

"How ironic," Andrea said. "Vanessa was obsessed with Paul and Tucker was obsessed with Vanessa."

"All of this sleuthing makes me want to eat something sweet," Lucy said. "What's for dessert?"

"I thought you weren't eating sweets anymore," Gloria teased.

"I'm going to make an exception, but only for today."

"I made cupcakes. I'll go get them," Gloria said. She sprang from her chair, walked over to the pantry and reached inside for the tiered arrangement of pink and blue cupcakes. She returned to the table and placed the cupcakes in the center.

"How cute," Dot gushed. "Pink and blue."

Lucy reached for a cupcake. "With sprinkles."

"Pink and blue." Rose, who was sitting on Andrea's other side, slowly turned. "Pink and blue."

Alice made a small choking noise.

Andrea cleared her throat. "I, uh, have an announcement to make. Brian and I are having a baby."

The room grew silent as all eyes focused on Andrea.

"A baby?" Lucy squeaked.

"We're having a baby," Margaret shrieked.

"We're gonna have a baby," Dot whispered.

Ruth slammed the palm of her hand on the top of the table. "I knew it! I mean, I suspected it."

All of the women began to talk at once and Gloria leaned back in her chair, grinning from ear-to-ear, all the while thinking this was going to be one pampered little bundle of joy.

The end.

If you enjoyed reading "Stranger Among Us," please take a moment to leave a review. It would be greatly appreciated! Thank you!

The Series Continues...Book 18 in the "Garden Girls Cozy Mystery" Series Coming Soon!

Get Free Books and More

Sign up for my Free Cozy Mysteries Newsletter to get free and discounted books, giveaways & soon-to-be-released books!

hopecallaghan.com/newsletter

Meet the Author

Hope Callaghan is an author who loves to write Christian books, especially Christian Mystery and Cozy Mystery books. <u>She has written more than 50 mystery books (and counting)</u> in five series.

In March 2017, Hope won a Mom's Choice Award for her book, <u>"Key to Savannah,"</u> Book 1 in the Made in Savannah Cozy Mystery Series.

Born and raised in a small town in West Michigan, she now lives in Florida with her husband.

She is the proud mother of one daughter and a stepdaughter and stepson. When she's not doing the thing she loves best - writing books - she enjoys cooking, traveling and reading books.

Hope loves to connect with her readers! Connect with her today!

Visit <u>hopecallaghan.com</u> for special offers, free books, and soon-to-be-released books!

Email: <u>hope@hopecallaghan.com</u>

Facebook:
<u>https://www.facebook.com/hopecallaghanauthor/</u>

Gloria's Breakfast Bomb Recipe

<u>Ingredients</u>:
1 tube refrigerated biscuit dough (8 count)
1 tbsp. butter
2 tbsp. diced green pepper
8 eggs
¼ cup milk
3 tbsp. chopped chives
8 slices of bacon, cooked and crumbled (can substitute cooked, crumbled sausage or diced ham)
1-1/2 cup shredded cheddar cheese
4 tbsp. melted butter
1 tbsp. poppy seeds
Salt
Pepper

<u>Directions</u>:
- Preheat oven to 375 degrees.
- Spray a large baking pan with cooking spray. Set aside.
- In large bowl, whisk together eggs and milk.
- In a large, nonstick skillet, melt 1 tbsp. butter over medium heat. Sautee chopped green peppers.
- Pour egg mixture into skillet with the chopped green peppers, stirring occasionally until reaching desired consistency.
- Season with salt and pepper.

- Remove from heat. Fold in chives (or green scallion)
- Flatten each biscuit round to about ¼" thickness.
- Top each round of dough with scrambled eggs, bacon (or meat) and cheese.
- Bring edges of the dough together and pinch to seal.
- Place on baking sheet, seam side down.
- Brush tops with melted butter. Sprinkle with salt and poppy seeds.
- Bake 20-25 minutes or until the biscuits are golden brown.
- Serve warm.

*Makes 8 breakfast bombs.

Made in the USA
Monee, IL
17 May 2020